Social Deception Murder

Mia Tenroc

Social Deception Murder by Mia Tenroc
© 2021 Mia Tenroc
ISBN: 978-1-944433-05-5 (paperback)

McToner Publishing Inc.
P.O. Box 37
Goldenrod, Florida 32722
McTonerPublishing@gmail.com
www.miatenroc.com

All rights are reserved. This book, or any portion thereof may not be used or reproduced without written permission by McToner Publishing or the author. Any scanning, uploading, and distributing of this publication without the permission of the publisher is illegal and punishable by law.

This is a work of fiction. Names, characters, places, and incidents either are the product of the author's imagination or used fictitiously. Any resemblance to actual person, living or dead, business establishments, events, or locales is entirely coincidental.

If you purchase this book without a cover, you should be aware that this book is stolen property. It was reported as "unsold and destroyed" to the publisher, and neither the author nor the publisher has received any payment for this "stripped book."

Permission:
ID 48861273 © Anton Petukhov / Dreamstime.com – Front Cover Photo
ID 1388444 © Svetlana Kashkina / Dreamstime.com – Back Cover Photo
Cover & Formatting by Eric Cornett
Author's photo by Ivy Neville Photography

Abletown

Chapter 1 – Mr. Greenson's Story (Saturday)

"MURDER, I tell you! It was the same as if he held a gun to her head!" Mr. Greenson was so angry that he was red in the face.

Alan looked surprised and worried. His best friend, Jake, runs a funeral parlor and at times Alan would help him out since Jake had no partners or spouse. There was a couple of good employees but in this case, they still needed the extra manpower for lifting the casket when they would take it to the gravesite at the cemetery next door. Besides Mr. Greenson's apparent high blood pressure, he didn't seem strong enough to do the task.

SOCIAL DECEPTION MURDER

All of the encouragement Mr. Greenson needed to continue his story was for Alan to simply nod his head. "This con artist found my mother online on a dating site for elderly singles. Mom was happily married to my father for 50 years when he was struck down with a heart attack. For over five years, Mom was content just doing things with the family. Then, a friend of hers used this site and met a very nice man, someone she could go to dinner and theatre plays with. I admit that it was nice for her friend to have a companion, but after Mom saw her friend's happiness, she started longing for someone to share adventures with. She didn't want to remarry or anything serious, but she wanted that companionship. Well, this con man found her photo and story, and asked her out for a date. Mom knew not to let a stranger in the house, so she suggested meeting at a restaurant. Her friends went a little early and got seated to keep an eye on things. They snapped this photo catching Mom and the crook in the background." Mr. Greenson enlarged the photo so Alan could get a good look at the man. "He introduced himself as Mr. William Rogers. He pretended to be this great guy, but what he was really doing was using a good man's name to invoke comfort. He claimed to be retired military, Air Force. He said he now uses those flying skills of his to take food and medicine to people in Third-world countries, and that he even flew vital organs to their hospitals on occasion."

MIA TENROC

"Mom got caught up in his stories and enjoyed the hefty number of compliments and attention he gave her. My sensible mother fell for him big time. They dated about six weeks. Around that time, he started to complain that his plane needed work, but as soon as it was up, he would take her for a flight. Then a couple of weeks later, Mr. Rogers comes in looking so sad, claiming his daughter needed surgery but that the doctor and hospital wouldn't start until they got their copay of $1,500.00. He began crying, saying he wanted to be there for his daughter but that all his spare money went into the plane. He claimed to have investments but that it would take a few weeks for his broker to sell and get him the money. Supposedly, his daughter was in such critical condition that she might not make it that long. Being the good Samaritan she was, Mom lent him the money."

"Mr. Rogers never met the rest of the family, and he refused to get his picture taken with Mom. He didn't know about the one on the first date. I was on guard already because I felt those were warning signs that he might not be honest, but when Mom told me about the money, I jumped all over her. She defended him, saying he was a good person and gentleman. She claimed she wouldn't give him anymore and insisted that he meet the family so we could see for ourselves what a great guy he was. Two weeks after that, Mom came in crying and broken-hearted. William Rogers had to leave immediately to be with his daughter, and Mom gave him more money for the trip, hotel, and other expenses. Another $10,000.00 conned out of her. She realized he wasn't coming back after his phone was disconnected and he didn't stay in touch with her. After that, she had no energy to go on."

Some people entered the viewing room so Mr. Greenson rushed off to greet them and recite his story again. Jake came over to Alan, "Sorry about that. I should have warned you about the story. I appreciate you helping today."

Alan saw Mr. Greenson, phone in hand, telling the next group the same story. Alan responded, "That's ok. It appears to be how Mr. Greenson is dealing with the loss of his mother. He probably feels guilty for not protecting her more. Are we still on for dinner after the service? I know Naomi is looking forward to it."

Jake smiled, "My girlfriend, Stacy, is in town. It will be nice for the four of us to hang out again. She still wants me to sell this place and move to New York City with her, but I actually like being in a quieter town."

Alan pointed out, "Yes, but if you went there, you could pursue your acting desire."

Jake disappointingly replied, "I'm 6'7". Yes, I'm talented enough but I've been told too many times I make the others on stage look small. I'm limited on what roles I can play. After so many rejections, I don't want to get turned down again. I keep hoping she will get transferred somewhere else."

Alan stated, "You can still bury people in New York City if that's what you want to do. You can't pass up on love, and I can tell how much Stacy cares about you. Why don't you train someone to run the place and I can help keep an eye on things if you really want to go."

Jake had to go away since the service was about to begin. The place was filled with people there to mourn the life of Mrs. Greenson. Jake needed to worry about living life and not just helping other people say goodbye.

Abletown

Chapter 2 – Striking Again

Jake gallantly held out the chair for Stacy to sit in. Naomi cleared her throat. "What?" asked Alan. "Oh, I guess you want me to do that too." He did but Naomi clearly wasn't impressed since she had to force the issue.

Stacy asked Alan, "How is your mother, Jean? It was a shame she couldn't join us tonight."

Laughing, Alan answered, "Jean is on a date tonight. It's going to be a special one."

Naomi said, "She and Nick go out every Friday night. There isn't anything new there. Why didn't they join us?"

MIA TENROC

In a sly way, Alan replied, "I'm not supposed to tell, but I can't wait until tomorrow. Nick is going to ask my mom to marry him."

Jake questioned, "I thought they were already married. She wears a wedding band."

Alan clarified, "They got married in a church years ago, but my mother doesn't trust the institution of marriage so she wouldn't file the marriage license with the court. Besides, it would cut down on the Social Security benefits she would receive. Mom believes men change once you marry them, so she makes more money and keeps Nick in line better with not finalizing the marriage. I've been coaching him on what to say to get her to change her mind. I like Nick a lot and he is good for her."

After ordering the meal, the conversation turned to the stories that Stacy was covering on her job as a reporter. "I might be getting the offer for the Washington DC beat for the network. That would be a huge career move. I really like my work but I don't exactly love the rent situation in New York City. DC isn't much better but with the subway being so good there, I could live further out and get something more affordable."

Alan reminisced, "Mom and I have been to DC a couple of times. Once, we took a tour of the Capital Building. The guide asked questions throughout the tour and we answered every one of them. The guide then started to ask if anyone else on the tour knew the answer besides us. Since their answer was always no, he turned to us to answer the question, which we did. We were rewarded with a special tour that had the original Congress Hall, the original Supreme Court, and the meeting rooms. One evening, we took a walking tour about the night that Lincoln died, and it was done by an actor in character as a policeman. He described the buildings for what they were being used for at the time. It ended in front of the White House where we voted if the different people involved in the story were guilty or not. There is so much to do there. However, you don't get much food from the restaurants there for the price so it's better to eat in instead of going out. Hey Jake, you could do a role like that walking tour actor."

The reaction expected from Jake didn't match what Alan baited him for. "I don't believe it! Now don't turn suddenly, but I believe that's Priscilla across the room and the guy with her looks like the one in the picture Mr. Greenson showed us."

Alan turned slowing in his chair, trying not to look too direct. "Sure enough, it is Priscilla. I can't see the man's face enough to say."

Jake asked, "Can you check with Jean to see if Priscilla is seeing someone?"

MIA TENROC

Alan explained, "Priscilla moved out of the Friend's Home and no longer associates with Mom and her group of friends. She blames Mom, Aunt Josephine, and Belinda for the reason the mayor didn't get re-elected. That wasn't true, of course, since the mayor only got two votes. Even his wife and kids didn't vote for him. Still, if that is the man, I don't want to see anyone else getting ripped off. Did Mrs. Greenson live around here?"

"No, she lived in the east part of the state. She originally lived here but moved to be near her son. They had the service here because her husband used our funeral services and they wanted to be buried together. It would make sense for a con man not to work the same territory but to stay in the same state. He would know the laws and what he could get away with." Jake suggested, "Let's go check it out."

The two men walked up to the table unnoticed by Priscilla or the man. Priscilla was in the process of removing an envelope from her purse. "Good evening, Priscilla," said Alan. "By any chance does the package contain money to help pay for medical bills for this man's daughter? Good evening to you. Are you William Rogers?"

"Who are you? My name is Wilson Roberts. No one invited you to interfere with our dinner. Get out of here!"

SOCIAL DECEPTION MURDER

Jake explained, "There is a con artist that looks just like you, dating woman he meets on a singles site. Priscilla, did he tell you that he flies a plane and that it needs repairs and that's why he doesn't have the money to help his daughter?"

Priscilla's hand went to the table and snatched back the envelope. The man pleaded, "Please don't believe these crazy men. You and I mean so much to each other. I want to be with you, even if you can't loan me the money."

Priscilla walked off saying to Alan. "You and your mother can't stand to see me happy."

Alan spoke loudly after her, "I'm saving you, but you never could see the truth in any situation."

Abletown

Chapter 3 – Making it Final

It was a romantic evening, with the sunset creating many vibrant colors in the sky. Jean was sitting across the table gazing at the man she loves as they were having dinner by the water's edge. In his fifties, Nick Noble was still so physically appealing and strong, with a slim waist and broad shoulders. His dark blonde hair with piercing blue eyes rounded off the description of this really good-looking man.

"You're acting nervous tonight," Jean observed.

Nick reached across the table and took her hand. "I want you to marry me." He stated bluntly.

Jean held up her hand that had a wedding ring on the finger, "We're already married. We made our vows before God in the church, in front of our friends, two years ago. We are dedicated to each other. I hope you know my love for you is strong. I can't imagine ever being without you."

Nick knew all her arguments against filing the marriage certificate. "I want to make it all the way legal. I know you will say that it will cut into your income but Jean, you are already worth a lot of money, so it won't hurt you. I know you like being independent. I don't care if we change anything. You can still keep your apartment in the Friend's Home. We can be together on the weekends like we are now. Why are you so unwilling to make the final step?"

Jean responded thoughtfully, "I was married once. He treated me like a queen until the night of our wedding. He started bossing me around at the wedding reception. The next day, he said I was forbidden to see my family. Whenever I started to walk away from the marriage, he would act nice until he thought the threat was gone. If I did something to displease him, he would find a way of punishing me."

Nick kissed Jean on the cheek, "We have been together over five years now. You know me. Do you really think I'm going to change?"

Jean redirected the question, "Why does it mean so much to you if we file the marriage certificate?"

Nick responded, "First, I'm supposed to tell you that I'm more than willing to sign a prenuptial agreement."

"Who told you that?" Jean said laughing.

Nick looked sheepishly, "Alan. He pointed out that you liked controlling the finances. Since you started helping me with mine, I've increased my financial value by 5 times what it used to be. I know you lived through being poor and don't want to go back there again. But you know that I don't waste money. We are on the same page when it comes to spending. Your wealth will go to Alan or whomever you want if, God forbid, something happened to you. My money will be divided between my four children."

Jean nodded her head smiling, "So you and Alan are ganging up on me."

Nick continued, "My family knows about our half-marriage, in the church but not all the way legal. Timothy is getting married in about two weeks. I would like to make it legal before then. When we walk into the place, I want the world to know of our love and devotion to one another. I think my family views us as being there only partway for each other. I would be proud to have you on my arm as my full wife."

Jean was touched. "That is so sweet and sincere. I already view us as being totally devoted to each other, without the paper. If it means that much to you, I will agree to the full marriage." They kissed as the starry night surrounded them. It was like a scene from a movie.

Jean paused, "If we are going to be married, with you being a police detective and all, I think I should tell you; I was once suspected of murdering my ex-husband. I hope that doesn't have any effect on you or your job."

Nick looked surprised, "Why? Did you do it?"

Jean laughed, "No, I didn't kill him. Not that I was unhappy when it happened. He deserved it, after all. I think dancing on his grave and running a toy Corvette over it was why they considered me a suspect."

Nick stared, "That's very unique. I suppose you had your reasons for such an odd act."

Jean explained, "When we got married, he bought me a Corvette on the condition that I would give up riding my motorcycle. He put it in his name when he purchased it. He got mad at me one day for going to see my grandfather on his birthday, and when I got home, I found out that he sold the car as "punishment". I don't really want to talk about it as I would hate to ruin this wonderful evening but I feel if we are going to make our union legal, as a homicide detective, you should know the truth. It was a business partner that killed him for stealing company finances. I just wanted you to know about the arrest. Do you have anything to disclose?"

"In a sense, yes. Nothing as good as your story, though. I would like to hear the full story sometime later. I act like I get along with my ex-wife, but that's not my real feeling inside. You know that she got pregnant on purpose as a way to trap me. I took it like a man because I allowed it to happen. She kept having children even though I wanted to stop. She never worked and spent every dime I ever made. I was trying for a hockey career but gave it up to be there for my children. You know the story. My best friend from childhood, Kurt, got a huge amount of money after his wife died. He always wanted a large family but was unable to have kids. With me working 16-hour days to pay the bills, he was the stand-in father for baseball games and other family activities. Then the next thing I know, he and my wife tell me they want to marry. Even my children thought it was for the best. It relieved me of the financial burden because he had money. I did provide for my kids and paid for their college and other expenses, but the rejection by those I loved hurt me deeply. When we walk into the wedding, I will be the winner because I will have you. Your son, Alan, and his wife, Naomi, I consider my family too. I'm so glad they are going and willing to be by my side. I will be envied for making my life a success."

SOCIAL DECEPTION MURDER

Jean kissed him again. "Let's keep it simple this time. How about a wedding at the beach with Alan and Naomi standing there with us?" Nick was a very happy man.

Abletown

Chapter 4 – Wedding Plans (Sunday)

The next day, Sunday, Jean and Nick asked the preacher that married them in the church to do the ceremony the next day. He was scheduled to go out of town and couldn't do it. Jean suggested, "My sister, Jo, can legally marry people. Since we already married in the church, why don't we ask her?"

Nick agreed, "I didn't know that, but that's fine with me."

After the service, they walked to Josephine and Mike's house on Third Street. Nick asked, "We have decided to finish the marriage and file a license tomorrow. Will you do us the honor of officiating the ceremony?"

SOCIAL DECEPTION MURDER

Jo was thrilled to be asked, "When? Where? What is the plan?"

Jean, always the one to organize things, explained, "Tomorrow morning, when the courthouse opens, Nick and I will be there getting the license. I presume as my brother-in-law that you, Mike, will be attending as well. We will meet the two of you, Alan and Naomi at the Seashore Café. At the ceremony, we will be using traditional vows, have brunch at the café and then go file the certificate. I already talked to the kids and they are good with that schedule even though it means getting up early for them. Nick will be back to work by noon, and you and I can do our water aerobics."

"Sounds romantic." Jo said, "I hope you can tell I'm being sarcastic. You act like it's no big deal and it really is."

Nick assured her, "Believe me, I have an evening planned tomorrow night that will be plenty romantic, but you're not invited. Speaking of plans, we better go because Stacy is in town and we are headed to Jean's house, that Alan lives in, to cook dinner for them. Thanks so much for getting on board with this wedding on such short notice. I'm wearing a suit; Jean is wearing what she calls her Monet dress that's has a flower pattern of pastel colors. Just pick something you already have that works with that to wear because I presume you don't wear a robe. Mike, you can be the photographer so you can wear whatever you want."

Jean and Nick arrived at Jean's house to discover it decorated with wedding banners and signs of congratulations. Alan shook Nick's hand. "Welcome to the family, Dad. You told me last night was when you planned to propose so when I didn't hear from you, I assumed it all went well." Alan then went over and kissed Jean, "Mom, you are doing the right thing. I'm sure you won't regret this. Just confirming Nick's plan that the wedding is in the morning?"

Jean turned to Nick, "The two of you must have done a lot of talking behind my back."

Naomi added, "Last night, Alan was so excited about it that he spilled the story at dinner. Jake and Stacy will be here soon. In fact, here they are now."

Jake approached them with flowers, "I brought different kinds. We can make up something suitable for Jean to carry and a boutonniere for Nick to wear. I have all the material to wrap the stems. If kept in the refrigerator, they will be fine for tomorrow."

Jean insisted, "You must let us pay you for the flowers."

Jake shrugged his shoulders, "They would have been thrown away anyways. They are from a funeral we had today. I figure the flowers would appreciate being used for a happy event before they go."

Over the meal, Jake and Alan related the story about Mr. Greenson, his mother and the crook. "Is that illegal?" They asked Nick.

Nick replied, "In some states, it is. It depends on how you ask for the money. If you asked for the money based on a lie, you can be prosecuted, but if you indicate a need for money and the person gives it willingly, it is not. I take it that Mr. Greenson probably tried to pursue getting his mother's money back and was unsuccessful. If so, I assume that this Mr. Rogers, or whatever the man's name really is, did it in such a way as to not break the law. It is common for a confidence man to use fake names that sounds similar to their real name. You said his name was William Rogers, so he would pick a name with the "Will" sound in it and usually have the initials of the pseudonym match his real name. The fact he wouldn't meet the family and didn't want pictures taken is another sign of trouble. Unfortunately, there will always be crooks and victims. I take it from Priscilla's response that she will at least be on guard."

Jean suggested, "Priscilla still speaks to Fannie because she sees her at the senior center in town that Fannie manages. I will see if Fannie would be willing to talk to Priscilla to warn her."

The dinner was so filled with joy. There were many toasts and talk of a happy future.

When hugging goodbye to Jean, Jake whispered, "Alan seems to be the matchmaker lately. He keeps pushing me to move to be with Stacy. At least he got the victory with you and Nick."

Alan and Naomi gave hugs to Jean and Nick. "We will be there early tomorrow waiting for you. We will bring the flowers."

Abletown

Chapter 5 – The Wedding (Monday)

Josephine and Mike picked Jean up early to go to the wedding. She slipped into the back seat with a minimal "Hello".

Mike laughed, "You don't seem too excited. I thought you would be bouncing around in joy."

Josephine turned to look at her sister, "Scared?" Jean nodded yes as she sighed. "Don't be. If you were making a mistake, I would tell you so. I know the last marriage was a nightmare but after five years, if Nick had any kinks in his armor, it would have showed up by now."

After arriving at the restaurant, Jean sat on the back porch while Mike went in to get tea and coffee for them. It was a beautiful day: blue skies, white puffy clouds, the warm temperature cooled by the breeze coming off the ocean that made curls in waves on the shore. The chiffon of Jean's dress floated as she walked, with the color patterns making her look like a walking flower garden. Jean stared at the water without a smile. She looked at Josephine and asked one more time, "Are you really sure it's the right thing? He did sign a prenup, so the most I'm out of if things don't go well is just another piece of my heart."

Josephine tried to look mad at Jean, "Snap out of it right now. You should be happy."

A smile came to Jean's lips. Josephine thought, 'I got her thinking right.' But then she realized Jean was looking past her, watching Nick get out of his car. Jean turned "You're right. When I see him, I can't help but smile. Thanks for the support and getting me here." She gave Josephine a quick hug as she started walking toward Nick, who was running to meet her.

Suddenly, other cars started arriving: Stacy and Jake, and then Janice, Nick's partner on the force. Even Nick's boss showed up to the wedding. He reluctantly approached them, "I guess if I can't get rid of you, Jean, I might as well be embracing the day with you."

Josephine took charge, "Since this isn't a normal wedding, let's all grab chairs and make an aisle. Nick, why don't you walk in with Naomi and each of you take your spots. Alan, you take Jean's arm and walk her down the aisle to give her away to Nick, then move to the best man's spot."

Alan held his mother's shoulders from behind, pointing her in the direction where Nick was waiting. The bouquet in her hands was shaking. "It's ok, Mom. You can do it. Nick is a great guy. This means so much to him, and you want him in your life. You have nothing to lose here and I gain a great dad that I never had before."

Jean responded in a very quiet voice, "I know. I know. You're right. I've seen so few good marriages in my life but I'm hoping this will be one of them."

Alan continued his pep talk, "Doesn't he back you up whenever a murder happens around you? He never complains about anything, really. He loves you for who you are. You have a lot of money, but he always pays, so he's not using you."

"Alright. I'm ready." Jean took a couple of shaky steps across the beach area to the flower garden where Nick was waiting. Mike was taking pictures as were many of the other guests. Jean noticed another camera man and realize it was Dave Smith, who took pictures at the crime scenes for Nick. She started to laugh. "Dave, should we be lying down when we take our vows so you have your more normal poses?" Naomi was giving a small wave of encouragement.

Dave laughed, "Maybe we should smear catsup on your dress to make it more like my job. On second thought, I think I can handle it with people standing upright."

Nick took Jean's hand, leaned over and gave her a kiss on the cheek. "I thought you were going to run."

Jean was trying to control her nerves. "I want you in my life always, so I'm willing to risk this."

Nick whispered, "You are so romantic, saying such sweet things." Jean knew he was being sarcastic, but she asked for it so she let it go. She turned to Jo, "I'm ready."

Jo said the standard words used at a wedding, and then Nick and Jean each expressed their appreciation for one another.

After the kiss, when walking down the aisle, Jean asked, "A crime scene photographer, Nick?"

He chuckled, "I've gotten many convictions from his great pictures. Who better for the job? He was glad that I invited him. He prefers to photograph the living."

When mingling with the guests, Jean ended up talking with Janice and the boss. "I'm surprised you came but I'm glad you did. I promise to try not to bring too many murders your way."

SOCIAL DECEPTION MURDER

After the meal, when everyone was to go about their day, Jean turned to Nick, "Be careful and hurry home."

Nick tried to act surprised, "Don't tell me you're changing so soon after the marriage and starting to tell me what to do."

They all left laughing.

Abletown

Chapter 6 – News in the Pool

Jean, who usually did the calling during water workouts, said, "Let's start with our usual three jogs: run in place, wide leg jog, and kick the heels to the side. Watch for my change because we have important matters to discuss when working out today. Some of you were there but for those that weren't, Nick and I officially got married today."

Belinda complained, "How could you do that and not invite us?"

Fannie responded, "We were at the last ceremony, and how many weddings can you go to for one couple?"

Jean ignored the verbal teasing and continued, "Nick and I are leaving on Thursday for his son's

SOCIAL DECEPTION MURDER

wedding on Saturday so why don't you decide who will lead the calls in the pool. Switch to jumping jacks, then go to cross country ski."

Josephine was nominated to lead the class. Belinda said, "I need to talk and not keep count of how many moves we are doing. Say what Jean? Go to twist and rocking horse now? Got it."

Jean continued, "I have big news about Priscilla." After telling the story of Mr. Greenson, his mother, and the dinner where Alan and Jake tried to save the ungrateful Priscilla, she opened the floor for discussion.

Josephine started, "That makes me so mad. We need to somehow teach that man a lesson. It should be illegal. I wish we knew more about what makes it legal and how we can get him to do something to put him into jail."

Fannie suggested, "Why don't we get Eve to talk to Priscilla? She appears to still be friends with her."

Belinda cringed at having to deliver bad news. "Eve lost her job, again. She can't afford to keep up two homes. She placed the one in town up for rent and moved to the farm with her husband and his junk. It's a 45-minute drive each way so she won't be joining us for a while."

"I guess that leaves me," said Fannie. "I think Priscilla will listen to me. I will call her and see if I can visit. I might be able to make her realize the danger of being with that man. I will find out how she got hooked up with him and report back."

Belinda suggested, "One of us should go undercover to catch him. I would do it but I don't know if I have the acting ability to pull it off. Do you remember Klaus and Deanie, the acting couple that worked with us on the Royal Wedding Funeral? Do you think they would meet with us and make suggestions?"

After an hour in the pool, Jean got out and called Jake to see if he thought Deanie and Klaus would meet with them. She told him that they wanted to stop the man from conning anyone else. Jake approved of the idea to at least meet with them. A half hour later, Jean received a call, "I'll put this on speaker. We are still all sitting around the pool."

Jake told the ladies, "Deanie and Klaus would love to help out. Have everyone that wants to help meet here tomorrow night. Jean, can you bring Nick or Janice here to give us legal advice?"

"Sounds like a plan except for having the police there. We will contact them after the meeting if needed, but Nick would try to stop me from taking action," responded Jean. "Thanks for getting on board with this.

SOCIAL DECEPTION MURDER

Can you check to see if Mr. Greenson contacted the police and what they told him?"

Abletown

Chapter 7 – Plotting the Reverse Con (Tuesday)

Jake took the lead at the meeting. He reiterated the information he had received from Mr. Greenson. "The family did indeed go to the police asking for help, which only embarrassed and upset her further. She would have preferred to have just lost the money than to admit to being fooled. The reason why no legal action could be taken was because "Mr. Rogers" himself never asked for the money. He told his sob story, shed some tears and said things like, 'I don't know what to do.' The compassionate Mrs. Greenson was the one who suggested that she loan him the money. That's why it wasn't illegal. If he had asked her for the money, it could have been considered a criminal act. This man clearly knows the law and how to get around it."

Fannie spoke next. "Mr. Greenson sent the picture to Jake. I showed the picture to Priscilla. She is very angry about someone trying to use her but understands now what a favor Alan and Jake did by coming to the table that night. She gave me the website that she used. We downloaded her ad, his ad, and their letters to each other. I went through them looking for key words to use. Priscilla took down her listing, but his was still up last time I checked. She wanted to put a warning under the comments section and contact the site coordinator, but I talked her into waiting a few days until we decided what action we needed to take. She agreed but demanded that I report back to her. I tried to talk her into coming to the meeting, but she refused."

Jean stood up and reported, "I'm leaving in two days, so I can't be the lead on this. Alan and Naomi are also going to the wedding. We need a plan and someone to lead it. Any suggestions or volunteers?"

Josephine answered, "I'm mad as hell over this injustice and would be glad to take the lead, but I'm not exactly sure what we can do. What about keeping tabs on him on all dating websites and keep putting up the warning?"

Deanie spoke, "I think we should have someone go undercover. Do a reverse sting, an idea that came from a play we did years ago. Did the same one come to your mind, Klaus?"

Klaus nodded his head yes, "This is a real old one so we would need to update it. Men like this go after older woman that are newly single and might have inherited money when their spouses died. They go after someone looking for companionship. The fact they stayed married for so long shows dedication and compassion. That's what they look for. In the old story, they used a check scam to pull money from the crook's account, but no one banks that way today. A man once told me that he traded money for a living. This isn't exact on the countries but just as an example, he would first buy peso, then trade for the pound, and then trade that for yen. The rate of exchange isn't always the same for each country, so if you trade in a certain order, you can actually make a profit. Again, I don't know if that is true, but neither would the con artist. If we can find victims of this man, we could help get their money back."

Deanie asked, "Does anyone want to be the one to go undercover? Let's set up a table. Klaus can play the confidence man, and we will see which of you can act out the part of the reverse con."

After the test, Klaus and Deanie conferred in secret. Deanie announced, "I know this isn't the real thing but Gwen, you giggle too much. Josephine, your

SOCIAL DECEPTION MURDER

words were right but there was an anger and determination in your eyes that you couldn't hide. Belinda, you're over obliging and not quite protective enough. Fannie, your delivery is way over the top. Another thing I noticed is that all of you look too young and outgoing. This man will be looking for someone that's older, humble, shy, and a little stupid so he can fool them. Klaus and I discussed which person would be best to do the task and if you agree, we feel it has to be me."

Belinda laughed, "Standing there dressed in leopard skin print and leading this plan disqualifies you, but I know you are a great actor and can change yourself. Are you sure you want to do this?"

Deanie appreciated the irony of her real personality and the character she planned to be. "Actors are sort of like con men. They get you to believe they are something that they are not. I really feel my experience and insight into some plays gives me the advantage over this man. I want to do it if you approve."

The approval was unanimous. Josephine then took the lead. "We can't ever trust this criminal alone with Deanie. Whenever they have a date, two of us should be in the room with her. We will be stationed a few tables away and dressed in such a way as to not draw attention. We can talk our husbands into helping out. I think whenever possible we should have a man and woman watching. The man will be ready just in case anything dangerous happens and if Deanie needs help, she can signal the woman to meet her in the restroom. Fannie, since you're not married, you will be with Klaus."

"I win on that one," Fannie replied happily. "I know it is just pretend but it will be nice to have a stud on my arm." She slipped over to be near Klaus. "Will we look like a couple if I snuggle with you like this?"

Deanie came over and removed Fannie's arm from Klaus, "You'll call too much attention to yourself doing that. Try to act like a married couple that takes care of the flirting at home."

Belinda volunteered, "Why don't we work on the ad to be placed on the website for Deanie. I will then check for his picture on other websites that are for older single ladies. If this man's picture doesn't appear, I will contact the site to see if he had ever used them. I will be honest and tell them we are looking for people who fell prey to this con, like Mrs. Greenson did."

Josephine suggested, "Belinda, if the task is too much then make a list of the various sites so we can divide it among us. That way we can help too. Let's work on the tasks assigned and I will set up a private mass communication media site for us to post our findings and keep everybody informed as things develop."

Abletown

Chapter 8 – The Trap Begins (Wednesday)

Deanie, Klaus, and Belinda began working on the ad. Deanie, now known as Della, has been a widow for about 5 years. Since Deanie already looked 15 years younger than her actual age of 90, she had just the right physical appearance with minimal makeup. A head shot was done with her in a light blue dress that covered in a modest way with a gold cross around her neck. This projected her humbleness and goodness while also flattering her reddish blonde hair and blue eyes. Her address was not supposed to be included in the ad so to project wealth, they took the picture in front of the largest house in Abletown, which was Belinda's. No street name or address number was shown so they felt it was safe. They made sure to state that Della was looking for companionship.

After uploading the ad to the site, they searched for Wilson Roberts. Grateful that Priscilla hadn't put a warning yet on the account, they contacted Wilson as being interested. He responded within 15 minutes. He saw Della was new and reacted quickly, thinking she might be a good catch. Dinner was arranged for that night at 7:00. Deanie was amazed at the fast turnaround.

The entire group was contacted, and Josephine arranged for Fannie and Klaus to be the first to watch from a distance. Klaus, who was originally all for the sting, started to worry about the safety of his wife. Deanie, still determined to go through with it, told him, "Relax. I already agreed that I won't leave the house without the company of the other group members for protection."

That night, when Deanie entered the restaurant, she walked with grace and shoulders back but not with her head held too high and certainly not with overconfidence. Wilson was certainly impressed, "You're more beautiful than your picture. I'm a very lucky man to have your company for dinner tonight." He held out her chair, ordered cocktails and looked over the menu.

MIA TENROC

Deanie as Della said, "I love your selection of restaurants. I haven't gone out much since my husband died. I'm a good cook but if I do order out, I usually take it home to eat. I dislike eating alone in public." Wilson leaned forward showing interest. 'Darn,' thought Deanie, 'This guy is a good actor. The leaning in projects inclusion.'

He responded, "I'm surprised you don't date more often. I would imagine you having plenty of friends."

Deanie explained, "I do have a lot of female friends, but most of them are married. I feel like a third wheel if I go with them, even if they say it isn't so. I've not really been interested in male companionship because it takes a while after a loss of a loved one to be ready to move on. Your ad sounded like you felt the same way, which is why I clicked on it. We will have to tell our history to each other I suppose, so we might as well get it over with. How long have you been single?"

Wilson told his well-rehearsed story. "My wife has actually been gone for about 10 years now. I was in the military, an Air Force pilot. Wanting to do something important in my life, I bought a plane when I got out. I began working with a non-profit that delivers medical supplies and food to impoverished people. I also work with hospitals delivering organs for transplants. There is a short time in which you can remove an organ and

SOCIAL DECEPTION MURDER

send to the benefactor, so often private planes do the work on the spur of the moment. I'm proud to serve others like I have my whole life. I'm not a rich man because I only get paid what they can afford to give me. If the insurance company pays for the organ transfer, I accept the payment. But if the recipient doesn't have insurance, I don't charge them. Now it's your turn."

Deanie did the proper smile and oohs and aahs over his story. "I'm afraid mine isn't near as exciting. Like I said on the ad, I've been a widow for five years. My husband did investments and let's just say he did alright but not wealthy. I learned a lot from him. He didn't leave much because his illness ran through our savings, but with the knowledge he gave me over the years, I've been able to invest the remainder and have now built my own nest egg. I spend my time working at the church and other volunteer jobs. Even if I could get a real job at my age, I don't think I would want it. When you volunteer, you can take off whenever you want. I do alright for myself. Say, why don't we do a quick list of favorites, like places to travel to, songs, movies and so on. That would help us know what we have in common."

He agreed to that and the conversation turned to cheerfully listing all the things they liked. Deanie didn't have to lie or pretend on this portion so it made it easier.

MIA TENROC

Klaus was sitting across the room with Fannie. He sat facing the table so they wouldn't be caught turning or staring. Fannie was easy to spot in a crowd with her blonde, thick hair that turned heads and with having one blue eye and one green eye. She tried to keep her voice quiet to not draw attention. Klaus would describe what motions and reactions were happening at the table of interest. Fannie felt the need to reassure Klaus that Deanie was smart and could handle it. "I am physically strong due to lifting furniture at my secondhand store, Fannie Annie's Attic, and could easily punch the guy out if he did something wrong." That brought out a laugh from Klaus, but she really did mean it.

Outwood

Chapter 9 – Arriving in Outwood (Thursday)

Nick, Jean, Alan, and Naomi had a nice, uneventful flight. They rented two cars since Alan and Naomi had to leave a few days earlier. Due to owning their own business, getting time off was difficult for the two of them. They did have loyal employees; most had been there since the day their business opened. Jake offered to stop by the store a couple of times a day to make sure everything was going smoothly, since Alan regularly returned the favor for Jake. Jake certainly knew little about video games, just like Alan knew nothing about embalming people, but business is business and they both were good at it.

MIA TENROC

Their final destination was a couple of hours drive to the north woods of Minnesota where Nick was born and raised. The town of Outwood was small, roughly the same size as Abletown where Jean grew up. It was the type of town where everyone knew each other's business. Nick stated in case Jean forgot, "I grew up with two best friends. Kurt, who is now married to my ex-wife, lives in the house I bought when I got married. Directly across the street is my other boyhood friend, Brian, and his wife, Anita. Brian wanted us to stay with him but that is too close for my comfort. I had the excuse that there wouldn't have been enough room for Alan and Naomi as well. We will be staying at this charming inn on Main Street. It was once a private home of the town's richest man but is now a hotel and restaurant. It's a good place for a honeymoon. Tonight, Brian and Anita will join us for dinner at the inn. I am glad you are with me for when we go to the rehearsal dinner tomorrow." He reached over and took Jean's hand. "I know how to keep a poker face, and I can hide the negative thoughts about my ex. I'm sure things will go fine this weekend. I'm looking forward to spending time alone with my grandchildren the week after the wedding. We can go to the Mall of America. There is so much to do there. I love my kids, don't get me wrong, but the grandchildren are much more fun when their parents aren't around."

SOCIAL DECEPTION MURDER

At dinner, Brian said some encouraging words about Timothy. "He is the finest young man and his bride, Violet, is just perfect for him." Unsure how much Alan and Naomi knew about Timothy, he added a point which he wouldn't have if speaking to Nick alone. "They both have Down Syndrome but it's mild. Tim is a good, hard worker on the farm. Fred and Iris treat him like he was their own child. Don't say anything because I'm not sure who knows, but they plan to leave their farm to him in their will. Things can always change, and I'm not sure if they've told Tim yet. Violet is the only heir to her parents, who are both pretty up there in age. She was a surprise baby. Her father is getting too old to farm so they are taking government money for not planting. They turned the barn into a wedding venue. Here in the north woods, it's all the rage to have your wedding in the barns. They are so proud they could have a wedding on their own barn for their own daughter. Violet is very good at helping plan the weddings. She is really smart at math and does all the bookkeeping. Those kids have a bright future ahead and they deserve it."

Nick responded, "I've talked to Timothy almost every night lately. He acts like he's not as hurt over what his mother did, but I'm not believing it."

Brian expressed his disgust for Sylvia. "I never know how that woman thinks. To not be happy for your son finding love is just wrong. She claims that she opposed the marriage because she wants to protect him. He was crushed that she said that people with disabilities shouldn't marry. Tim and Violet don't plan to have any children, but they can still enjoy life together. And they should! I would say Tim is trying to hide his emotional pain, but he isn't really speaking to his mother. You and I talked him into permitting Sylvia to come to the wedding, so I hope we didn't make a mistake."

Nick replied, "Tomorrow should be an interesting day."

Outwood

Chapter 10 – Moving Quickly

Jean called Josephine while Nick was in the shower. She felt a little guilty not telling her husband about the group's plan to stop the con artist, but she knew he would never approve. Besides, she wasn't doing it, Josephine was. Yes, she knew about it but that's not the same thing, she justified to herself.

Josephine said, "I'm so glad we have a burner phone for Deanie to use. I'll admit to worrying about what the creep would do to her if he knew what we were doing. Fannie and Belinda just walked in. Let me put this on speaker."

"I don't have long to talk so please give me all the facts as quick as possible," Jean warned.

Josephine started, "He called asking for another date. He said that Della's company was so soothing and enjoyable that he wondered how quickly they could get together again. Deanie didn't want to look like she was rushing things, and she also wanted to give us more time for our research, so she agreed to meet tomorrow night. He suggested going to a play at the Shakespeare Playhouse."

Belinda inserted, "I already had tickets to the play, so Steve and I will be the watch party."

Fannie added, "Belinda and I have been active on the websites. So far, we found 4 other victims. He still has his profile up on three sites with no feedback about the date on any of them. I think most of the women he used are like Mrs. Greenson and don't want to come forward.

Josephine explained, "We have set up a Facebook account that is private, and all the ladies are posting information there. We hope that will give us some help. They are looking for other victims. I'm not sure what we are going to do when we get all our information. I guess we will get in touch with the police or an attorney to find out the next steps."

Jean said quietly, "Nick's coming out of the shower. I better go. Call or text me if something happens because tomorrow night, we will be out late. Love you all and stay safe."

SOCIAL DECEPTION MURDER

Nick came out of the bathroom, "Who was that?"

Jean tried to look innocent, however you do that, "Oh, it was just Josephine checking in to see if we arrived ok."

Nick asked, "You love all of her?"

Jean just shrugged, "Fannie and Belinda were visiting with Josephine."

Nick studied his wife, "I know when you are deceiving me, and this is one of those times. Are you going to tell me what you are up to?"

Jean answered defensively, "I'm not up to anything. I'm here with you."

Outwood

Chapter 11 – Sylvia's Insult (Friday)

The dinner was to be held at the same place as the wedding on Violet's family farm. Nick and Jean had ordered the dinner from the best restaurant in Outwood. Since Timothy was so popular, they were all too glad to prepare the dinner. They offered to do it for free, but Nick insisted they let him pay. It was probably a discounted price but they made sure to include everything so it would be perfect.

Nick explained Brian's statement to Alan and Naomi as they rode to the farm. "Violet never came to town much. She was home-schooled, and as you can tell from the drive, it is really out here. Timothy grew up here in Outwood. He went to school even though they had to create special classes for him. Tim is always so happy and cheerful. He didn't let his disability hold him back one bit. He played hockey, like his father, as well as baseball, which he preferred. Kurt took him to all his games. I admit that he was a great dad to all my kids. Brian also had a very close relationship with Tim. He spent hours helping him perfect his game. There were times Tim wanted to ask for advice and knowing that Kurt would likely tell his mother, he would go to Brian instead."

"When Tim told his mother about the marriage plans, he was alone with her. After she told him no and why he shouldn't do it, he left. She didn't know it, but he pulled down the street and went back to Brian's to talk to him. He was very upset. Brian listened and thought they should go over and talk to Sylvia. In the meantime, John, my second son, and Sarah, my daughter, arrived. They were in the kitchen talking and didn't hear Brian and Tim when they came in the front door. Sylvia said some mean things, like disabled children shouldn't marry, that Tim wouldn't be able to handle it, and that Tim didn't think things through. Sarah agreed with her. John didn't say much but he also wasn't coming to his brother's defense. Brian and Tim silently left, with Tim's face covered in tears. The others never knew the two of them overheard their conversation. Brian called me immediately. Jean was on the phone too. We assure Timothy that he should marry if that's what made him happy. We told him that his mother was absolutely wrong and that he could handle anything that came his way. He was smart and had put a lot of thought into it. We said we would be there for him in any way we could. Tim felt a little better after the call. Sylvia told Kurt about Tim's marriage plans when he got home. Kurt called Tim, told him that he supported his decision, and assured Tim that Sylvia would be ok with it."

Naomi lamented, "That is a really sad story. I'm so glad we came to be by Timothy's side. How could anyone not love Violet? When they came down last time, we really enjoyed the visit. They loved our store and were so much fun to hang out with. I know the gift we brought them isn't practical, but he and Violet will have a blast. I didn't know then that they were more than just friends."

Alan asked, "What does your oldest son, James, think about the wedding?"

Nick replied, "He's all for it and called his brother to say so. They never admitted it but I think James and his wife have problem with Sylvia as well. They moved to a bigger city claiming it was for job opportunities, but I know they almost never come back to visit. The few times James does come to visit, he always stays with his best friend from high school even though there is room with Sylvia, and also in his brother and sister's homes."

SOCIAL DECEPTION MURDER

Timothy and Violet were standing in the driveway waiting on them. The joy of the greeting and hugs were wonderful. Violet exclaimed, "Thank you so much for agreeing to be my bridesmaid, Naomi. It means so much to me."

Naomi promised, "Tonight, I have three ideas for hair styles and makeup for you to try. You're beautiful the way you are but as a makeup artist, I want to give you options. This will be so fun."

Tim tugged at Alan's arm. "My house is just across the field. I got a new wide-screen television and some games I want to show you." The four took off for gaming fun.

Jean shouted after them, "Only look at what he has and then come right back here. The food is hot, and we will begin eating when everyone arrives."

Brian, who was to be the best man, was already there with Anita. Violet's parents, Larry and Marie, came out. Introductions were made. It only took minutes to set up the meal.

Marie said, "Thank you both so much for all that you are doing for Tim and Violet. I'm a little protective because she hasn't been away from home much but because of our trust in you, she will enjoy a honeymoon where there are theme parks, beaches and adventure when they use your condo. I'm glad Alan and Naomi will be traveling with them at times for their honeymoon."

"Jean and I are on our honeymoon as well. It's good they can use my condo for theirs. With Naomi and Alan nearby checking on things, they will be fine. My place is great for relaxing and being alone."

Brian asked, "Do you mean you two made it legal? I know Jean felt that getting married in a church was enough."

Nick put his arm around Jean, "Yes, we are spiritually and legally man and wife." He gave her a quick kiss.

Outwood

Chapter 12 – Rehearsal Dinner

Attending the wedding rehearsal and the dinner to follow were the wedding party, parents, and Nick's three other children. Last to arrive was Kurt and Sylvia, pulling up in a new Mercedes with temporary tags. Kurt didn't try to hide his anger. Sylvia waited in the car for him to open the door but after Kurt got out of the car, he walked straight over to greet Nick and Jean, and then the other friends. Sylvia got out of the car pretending that she was carrying items to cover up Kurt's faux pas.

Iris opened, "We did have a small shower for Violet with a few friends and neighbors, but I like Jean's idea of having one tonight after the meal so that she and Naomi could participate. James, John and

Sarah, we are so glad you could join us for the extra shower."

James explained, "Our spouses and kids will be here tomorrow. Since we are having the bachelor and bridal parties after the rehearsal, we thought it best to leave them at home for tonight."

The Pastor started, "I believe this is where I should be standing. Marie, where do you normally have the groom and best man come in? Ok gentlemen, please walk that way. I see the maid of honor ready to come down to the platform. Now, the bride and father." Everyone walked to their positions. He continued, "I just want to say that I've known Violet all her life. It is such an honor to do the service. I see Alan taking the pictures and getting the angle right for tomorrow. Will the music be on tape or live?"

Marie answered, "We have Lion's Music System doing the music for tomorrow. They have provided the music for many weddings that have been done in this barn. They know what to do, so while we don't have the music now, I'm sure it will go smoothly tomorrow."

The Pastor continued, "You have chosen the traditional vows. Do you Timothy or Violet plan to share any special vows or comments?"

Timothy was the one to reply, "We are afraid of being too nervous. I will just stay with the plan and if we decide to add any comments, we will do so before the first dance."

"Good plan. Are there any more questions? Let's walk through it one more time really quick. Very good, I think we have it. I'm going to beg off on the meal tonight because I have another engagement, but I do plan to stay tomorrow to enjoy your big day. My wife and I thank you for the invitation." With that, he departed.

Marie instructed, "I have the long table for us to sit at tonight, so the rest of the area stays clean and intact for tomorrow. Here is the food table that Nick and Jean have provided. Please let me know if you need anything further. Let's begin with Timothy and Violet going first on the food line."

Timothy finished his meal, and while the others were still eating, he got up and made an announcement, "Violet and I want to thank all of you for coming tonight and supporting us on this big occasion in our lives. Brian, thank you for being my best man. You have been there for me, my whole life in fact. Where is your daughter, Amber, tonight?"

Brian answered, "She will be here tomorrow. She is very happy for you and Violet. Tonight, she is out with friends from the high school because the dinner is usually for people in the wedding and family."

Anita asked, "What song are you dancing to for your first dance as bride and groom?"

Violet replied, "Unforgettable by Nat King Cole."

Sylvia said in a critical tone, "Why did you pick such an old-fashioned song? I guess I should have been available to offer advice throughout this."

Jean ignored her and cried out in such a sincere tone, "How wonderful. I remember the day Nick and I taught the two of you to dance the waltz. We went out dancing at the Crystal Palace that night. You two took the dance floor and even the professionals gave you a round of applause and told you what a great job you did. How romantic to dance to a song that means so much to you."

Violet said with a smile, "That was a moment I will never forget." Then she turned to Naomi, "Thank you so much for standing up with me, Naomi. You have acted like my best friend from the moment we first met. I'm so very glad we will actually be related after tomorrow."

Sylvia, who was trying not to speak to anyone, interjected, "You won't really be related."

Violet explained, "Not by blood, but by marriage. With Timothy being Nick's son, Naomi being Jean's daughter-in-law, and now that Nick and Jean are married, we will be related."

SOCIAL DECEPTION MURDER

Kurt cut in, "Did you two finally make it legal? I know you married in the church but held off filing the certificate for financial reasons."

Nick smiled, "I finally convinced her that we only need so much money and giving up that little bit isn't going to hurt us at all, so yes, we made it legal."

Alan added, "I was also pushing for it. Nick is like a father to me. Naomi and I love him and think he is perfect for Mom. After all, Mom needs to be married to a police investigator, since murder seems to follow her everywhere."

Sylvia added, "Kurt is also a policeman. He and Nick started on the force at the same time. Nicky just moved to the big city where there is more crime, unlike our peaceful loving town."

Kurt said to Nick, "We started at the same time, but your level of success is so much greater than mine." To Jean he asked, "Do you really have that many murders in your life?"

Jean replied while giving a hush look to Alan, "No." Meanwhile, Nick is nodding his head yes behind her back. Jean held up her wine glass, "Let's keep the focus where it needs to be. To Timothy and Violet."

Outwood

Chapter 13 – Bachelor Party

The men went with Fred to his farm, while the ladies stayed with Marie for their party.

Brian stated, "I wanted to make this party something that Timothy would like. He didn't want drinking and women because he only has eyes for Violet. I know he would prefer video games, which later he can do, but here is my list of activities. You can see Fred is setting up the campfire. Later we can snack on s'mores. We will have a watermelon seed spitting contest, then we will compete to see who can eat the rest of the watermelon wedge the fastest. Afterwards, we can have a rock toss contest. We can then share our best ghost stories around the fire." Brian opened the back of his SUV, "Here are the drinks and ice. I also brought tennis balls for the juggling contest. Let's start having fun."

Timothy was winning on all the contests. Brian intentionally picked things that Tim would excel in. Alan almost had him on the watermelon contest but they announced that Tim was the winner by having the cleaner piece with no red left at all. It didn't take long to complete all the games, so they did a couple of them twice. Afterwards, Timothy, James, John and Alan went to Tim's little house that was on the farm for some gaming. Larry and Fred started talking about farming and headed to the barn to look at some of the animals. This left the three friends alone around the fire.

Brian asked Kurt, "New car?"

Kurt couldn't suppress his anger, "Only for today. Sylvia started talking about getting a new car a few weeks ago. I went to the dealership over in Upland and told them that I would not pay for a new car. If they sold her one, they would have to find a way to get the money from her. We've done a lot of business with them over the years. They know me and my word. The word was NO. I will be seeing them tomorrow at the latest. There was nothing wrong with our old car."

Nick said, "I take it she has ran through all your money, the half million you got from the insurance company. You're still living in the house I purchased, so I'm assuming all the money was spent on material things for her."

Kurt turned to Nick, "What we did to you was really wrong. I now think I did the biggest favor for you in the world. I was enjoying your children and liked helping you since you worked two jobs to support them. Sylvia came on to me. She said I wouldn't get the time with the children because she loved me so much that it hurt her to see me and not be with me. Yes, you are right about the material possessions, one of the spare bedrooms is essentially a walk-in closet. She thinks she impresses the town with her fancy clothes, shoes, and cars. Hell, I'm working with boots that need to be resoled again. She trained up Sarah to be just like her. John isn't strong enough to stand up to her so he goes along with Sylvia's ideas. James can't really stand his mother, but he and I are still close."

Brian added, "I watched the reaction on Sylvia and Sarah's face when it came out that you and Jean are officially married. I think they are worried about their inheritance."

Nick laughed, "I signed a prenuptial agreement. Jean is the one with the money. Since she started helping me with my finances, I went from a value of about $50,000 to around $250,000. Jean knows how to handle money and never wastes any. She never told me how much she is worth, but just guessing, I would say well over a million easily. Her money will go to Alan if something happens to her. I placed mine in a trust and Jean is the trustee. That money will be split evenly between my four kids. Jean will be deciding when it can be given but I instructed on James, John and Sarah's portion to be used for my grandchildren's education. If I left it to my kids, Sylvia would try to get it. She never cared for anyone but herself."

Brian continued the hard questions, "Kurt, are you thinking about a divorce?"

Kurt replied, "I tried to get her to work. She doesn't even do charity work. No, she never worked a day in her life and still refuses to do so. Things will change at our house, starting tonight. If she wants a divorce, that's fine but who would support her? She isn't going to like the changes, but they will happen. I have a plan."

Outwood

Chapter 14 – Bridal Party

Being the bridesmaid, Naomi announced the plans for the party. "I want to do three makeup and hair designs and we can vote on what looks best. Let's start with a picture of you in your natural state." She took a few pictures of Violet. "I had to pack all my clothes in Alan's suitcase so this one could be for hair products, makeup, and the gift." She pulled out a Wonder Woman costume. "This first one is based on the movie so I thought it would be fun to have the whole outfit. Mom, Jean that is, is going to work on baking cookies so we can have a decorating contest. Of course, every one of them will be a winner but we will make up the category for each cookie." Naomi and Violet went into her bedroom for the transformation.

SOCIAL DECEPTION MURDER

Jean turned on music with happiness and celebration songs. Marie placed out the snacks and drinks. Sarah and Sylvia sat off in the corner of the room by themselves, making no attempt to be social.

Naomi emerged making the sound of a trumpet. "And for our first entry," Violet stepped out as her mother and Jean applauded. Violet said, "I didn't know I could look like this." She did look very good.

Naomi explained while taking several shots of the new look, "This one is a mature look. See how the arch on the eyebrow and simple lines of the hair is attractive but more blended?" They disappeared back into the bedroom.

Jean was laying out sprinkles, chocolate chips, various colors of icing in squeezing tubes, whip cream and other decorating items. She spread a sheet of newspaper with wax paper on top to create less mess for when they would work on the decorations.

A little while later, Violet emerged again. Her hair was in curls and pinned to flow down her back. Her makeup included more color. This time she was in a flowing dress with colors to match her face. Naomi had on the Wonder Woman costume. She explained to the others, "My husband and I run a video and gaming store. Our employees, Alan, and I enjoy dressing up in the costumes of the products in the store. We try to make it a fun place to work and visit. This look is a girly look that's fun." After more headshots, they disappeared in the room again.

Marie continued her attempt to engage Sylvia in conversation. Since they would both be parents of the couple, it would be better for them to get along for the couple's sake. Sylvia asked questions about the wedding business. Even though she didn't care about fashion, Marie politely talked about clothes, cars, and shopping.

Jean noticed how many stars were in the sky through the window, so she stepped out into the backyard to have a better view. She heard the back door open and, looking from the corner of her eye, watched Sarah walk over to her. "Jean, do you know why Violet chose Naomi over me to stand with her? Usually there is a bridesmaid and a maid of honor. Timothy didn't even speak directly to me tonight. Did I do something wrong?"

Jean responded, "I think you should talk to your father about that. I might be his wife, but that is an immediate family discussion."

Sarah was getting angry, "Maybe I should just march in there and confront Violet."

Jean flashed around, "You do not need to ruin her day! You know what you did. Just think."

SOCIAL DECEPTION MURDER

"If I knew, I wouldn't be asking. I have a right to be told the truth."

Jean decided rather than risk a scene to ruin the party, that it would be better to tell Sarah what she knew. "Remember the day that Tim told his mother about his plans to marry?"

"Yes, but Tim was gone before I got there, and I didn't talk to him about it."

Jean continued, "Tim was actually at Brian's house. He was very upset at his mother's rejection to the idea. Brian and Tim came back to the house to talk to Sylvia. When they came in the front door, you and James were in the kitchen talking with her. Think of the negative words that you said. You remember the conversation." Sarah was looking down, not at Jean. "Tim was very hurt at your words and you agreeing with your mother. He went to Brian's and called Nick. I heard how much you hurt him. We gave him the positive feedback and encouragement he longed for. Not just because that's what he wanted to hear, but because we believe in Tim and Violet both individually and as a couple."

Jean had noticed while she was speaking that Sylvia had slipped quietly out the back door. She was hiding on the porch believing the shadows covered her location but was close enough to hear the words.

Sarah tried to defend herself, "Mom was doing most of the talking. I might have agreed but you don't understand the verbal degrading that happens if we don't agree with her. Mom isn't someone you can talk to unless it's what she wants to hear."

Jean corrected, "You could have called Tim when you got away from your mother and gave him your support. Did you even call asking for him to bring Violet over for dinner so you could get to know her?"

Sarah shook her hear no, "What do you think I should do now?"

Jean advised, "Go in there and celebrate with her. Express your support but don't confront her directly or apologize until after the wedding. This is her time and day. Don't make it about yourself. The cookies are done. I better get in there."

She saw Sylvia hurry into the house. Again, Sarah didn't notice her mother. Inside, Violet stepped out for the third look, "The party look," exclaimed Naomi. Violet's hair was puffed out with curls, instead of being straight and contained. The makeup had sparkles and was very bold. More pictures were taken. Sylvia sat on the couch near the corner looking away. Sarah was up by Violet looking carefully at the pictures of the different looks.

"Naomi, you are a makeup genius. I wish I knew you when I got married. I would have loved this look."

SOCIAL DECEPTION MURDER

The ladies reviewed the four sets of pictures. Violet said, "I like my hair this way but feel the makeup isn't me. I hope I'm not hurting your feelings, Naomi."

"Not at all. That is why we have four options," Naomi replied.

Sarah and Marie pointed to the mature makeup look. "What about the mature makeup with the party hair, would that work? What is your favorite, Violet?"

Violet concurred, "I think it makes me look better than just normal, but I'm still looking more like myself and I love this hair. What do you think, Naomi?"

"That's why we are doing the tests tonight. I think the mature makeup and fun hair would look great."

Violet gave her a hug, "Thank you so much for being there for me."

Jean announced, "Now on to the cookie decorating." The preparations to protect the kitchen did little good as the kitchen got covered with toppings. At first, there was a degree of seriousness but after the voting of funniest, prettiest, most creative, unique design and most colorful, the whip cream and icing were getting smeared all over their faces. Naomi snapped pictures the whole time. Their makeup was ruined and they had to pull out towels to clean the sticky mess.

MIA TENROC

Marie noticed Sylvia walking to the front door. "Are you ok? Why not join the fun?"

Sylvia fought to keep the tears from spilling out, "I'm sorry to ruin the party. I have such a terrible headache." She glanced over her shoulder at her daughter and found that Sarah didn't even notice her leaving. Instead, the group was line dancing, laughing, and having a great time.

Kurt looked up and saw the new car pulling up the driveway. "What now? The party isn't supposed to end for another hour. It's only 9:00." He walked to the car and talked to Sylvia through the window. Walking back to the other men, they could see the irate look on Kurt's face, "Sylvia is claiming that she has such a bad headache that we need to leave. She only gets headaches when she doesn't get her way, or when someone gets the better of her, but I better go."

Outwood

Chapter 15 – The Long Ride Home

As soon as Kurt entered the car, Sylvia started crying. When Kurt didn't say anything or ask what was wrong, she said accusingly, "I don't believe you love me. I'm hurting and you just don't care."

Refusing to answer that, he simple replied, "I figure you will tell me what's wrong when you get done crying. What big injustice happened?"

That response angered Sylvia even more but she wanted to unload, "Sarah turned against me. I heard her tell Jean that if people don't agree with me that I make their life miserable." Again, no response from Kurt. "Why aren't you being supportive? I've been a good wife to you for years and you can't say anything. She agreed with me that my Timmy just isn't able to handle marriage. Now she is all over pleasing Violet." Again, no response. "Can you say anything?"

Kurt, knowing the fire this will cause, didn't care. His wife sneaked out and bought a car they couldn't afford. He just didn't care anymore. The kids would love him no matter if he was married to their mother or not. "I'm very happy for Nick and Jean. Nick doesn't know it for sure, but he thinks Jean is a millionaire. He deserves a nice, wonderful, and rich person after all we did to him."

The tears stopped and anger spilled out, "I'm much prettier than she is. Dark hair, no doubt dyed, a little overweight, not an exciting person to be around. Look at me. I have beautiful red hair, much thicker than her hair. I'm in perfect shape. I turn heads when I walk into a place. I project grace and high social standing. My parents were the richest people in town. I married below my class with Nick. You are lucky to have me." Again, no response. "I don't believe she is rich. Maybe I do, otherwise, why would he waste time with her? I think she is after his money to deprive my children of their inheritance."

Kurt responded, "They signed prenuptial agreements, so Nick's money goes to his kids. He told me he left his money in a trust with Jean being the trustee, but the money is to be used for the kids and grandchildren with her approval. He feels you would try to get the money through the kids and the trustee is to make sure not a dime goes into your pocket. We are all tired of your show, me included."

"You better hope I stay with you. After all, that new girl in town accused you of making a pass at her when you gave her that traffic ticket. Only having a good wife like me by your side and defending you will kill that talk."

Kurt's voice was angry, "That talk was killed because everyone knows me. They like and trust me. I didn't do anything wrong and the girl would be the last person in the world that I would want to be with. She is a sick person that manipulates others. She is cruel, the way she plays the students at the school against each other. This town is worse off because she is here. You aren't saving me. While you want to fight, let's get it all out. I told the dealership I wouldn't pay for the car. I sat in their office last week and told them how you won't work or contribute to the income. If they sold you a car, they could get their money back from you. As soon as we get home, I'm running over there to take this damn thing back. I hope they have our old car, or I will walk home."

Sylvia said, "It closes at 10:00. You will never make it there."

They pulled up in front of their house. "Get out! I'm going to try, and I will sleep in the guest room tonight." Kurt pulled away from the curb, almost taking his wife's foot with him as she jumped out of the way.

Outwood

Chapter 16 – The Party's Over

After Kurt left to drive home, Nick called Jean. "What happened? Sylvia was really ticked off."

Jean said, "I can't hear you. We are dancing to the song "Celebration". Let me go outside. I don't want to quiet down the fun." In the yard, Jean asked, "What did you say? Could you tell we are having so much fun?"

In a flat tone, Nick replied, "Yeah. That would be hard to miss. What brought Sylvia over here in tears?"

Jean made sure no one could hear as she briefly described what happened. "She was looking for a fight all night. She was very unfriendly and I'm just glad she decided to sneak off rather than ruin the party for Violet. I'm going back in now because that's what is important. Maybe that bit of the truth will wake her up.

No more wasting good party time talking about her. I'm going back in and will be over to pick you up at 10:00. I believe the car the kids came in is over there. I will drop Sarah off for her ride home."

The dancing, cookies, and whip cream fun continued. Sarah did notice her mother was gone and asked Jean about it. Marie overheard, "Your mother had a really bad headache and left."

Jean assured her, "Nick just called and said that she and Kurt left. I'm to drop you off at their party so you can ride home with your brothers."

At 10:00, the party ended. Violet was hugging Jean, "Thanks so very much for this party tonight, and for paying for the honeymoon. I'm so glad you are my mother-in-law." She hugged Naomi, "I'm so excited about tomorrow. I bet Tim will be so surprised when I walk down the aisle to meet him. I feel so special and pretty right now." She hugged Sarah, "Thank you so much for celebrating with me. I'm a good cook. Would you and your husband come over for dinner sometime?"

Sarah had tears as she replied, "I would like that very much."

When meeting up with the others, Sarah got out of the car and hugged her dad. "I'm glad you and Jean got officially married." She got into the car with her brothers as Nick and Alan piled into their car.

SOCIAL DECEPTION MURDER

Nick said, "Looks like you two had a lot of fun tonight." The women assured him that they did.

Alan exclaimed from the back seat, "What did you two do?" He was flipping through the pictures on Naomi's phone. "Whip cream faces?"

Naomi explained, "We got whip cream on our noses when eating the cookies so we had a contest to see who could lick the whip cream off from different parts of the face."

Jean showed a can of whip cream she had taken home with her. Nick's eyebrows rose. Jean suggested, "Why don't we look at the pictures and discuss our party later? How did your party go?"

Alan started telling all the details of the contests and that it ended with video games for four of them. "No surprises there," said Jean.

Alan expressed, "What? We enjoy games, and we had fun doing so."

Abletown

Chapter 17 – Anxiety at the Theatre

Klaus gave a small box to his wife as she prepared for her second date with Wilson. "You appeared to be doing fine the other night with your date with that undesirable crook. I kept watch for any sign that you might be in trouble. I admit that I'm worried about you." Deanie opened the box and gave an exclamation of surprise and appreciation. It was a leopard jewelry pin. "I bought this listening device from the spy store and took it to the jeweler. They mounted it on this pin behind the leopard's eye. I know you miss wearing your favorite leopard skin print clothes but that wouldn't match your character. Even though Steve and Belinda will be watching you tonight, I just couldn't stay home worrying. I will be sitting in a car a little distance away and I'll be able to hear everything that's being said. I would feel so much better if you wore it."

Deanie gave her husband a kiss, "I love the pin. I will feel better knowing you are near. Thank you." She dressed and they walked out to their cars to go to position.

Wilson waited nervously at the entrance to the play. He went on the dating site and saw that horrible Priscilla had left comments warning others to beware of him. She told how he tried to convince her to loan him money. He was trying to think through his situation. 'At least she didn't say any more about the other fake name or the accusations from the two men that I had conned someone else.' He took his profile down immediately. 'I probably should just move on. If Della doesn't show up tonight, that would probably be the best course. Move to another town or even another part of the state.'

Deanie walked up just then with a nice smile. "Hi. I hope I'm not late. You seem a little jumpy."

Wilson gave her a hug. "No, prefect timing. I have a tendency to be early. The military doesn't accept excuses for being late and while that was a long time ago, my habits never changed. I was concerned I was reading more into our last date than I should. I was afraid you wouldn't show up. I hope you don't mind my asking, have you been on the dating site and clicked on any more likes?"

Deanie shook her head no. "You were the only one I clicked on and when you responded so quickly, I didn't bother to search any other profile. Maybe I'm limiting myself, but we had so much fun last time, I wanted to go out with you a few more times. I never date multiple people and would prefer to see if we continue to enjoy each other's company before I date anyone else."

Feeling relieved, Wilson lied, "I felt the same way. The date was fun, and you are a wonderful woman. I even took my profile down. If this doesn't work out, I can always put it back up, but I would like to concentrate on our friendship. I guess we better go into the show." Wilson was glad he didn't have to do too much talking right then. He was more focused on the next steps of the game he was playing than the production.

Deanie was also thinking more than paying attention to the show. 'Maybe we had Priscilla put up the notice too soon. He was probably playing more than one person at a time. Giving the early notice would protect any other woman before they got hurt. He is acting like a trapped tiger with his pacing. Did I play my wording right outside? Yes, I think I did.' It seemed safer coming here but she noticed too many faces of

SOCIAL DECEPTION MURDER

people that she and Klaus knew. She decided to signal Belinda at the first intermission. She felt it was best to leave the theatre early.

Deanie met up with Belinda in the restroom as planned. She expressed her concern that someone might identify her in front of him. Belinda suggested, "He hasn't looked at the play once. Make it about him. Ask if he wants to go. I wouldn't say something like you have a headache. Keep it about him."

Halfway through the second act, Deanie leaned over and whispered. "You haven't been paying any attention to the play. You seem very distracted. Do you want to go? We don't have to end the date but just go get coffee somewhere."

Wilson whispered back, "But you said this was one of your favorite plays. Aren't you enjoying it?"

Deanie replied, "Yes, but I'm more concerned about you. I've seen the play multiple times in my life. I'm more concerned about what makes you happy."

They got up and left before the second intermission. Wilson was worried about rushing the game, but he hadn't hidden his upset too well. He wouldn't talk about money yet, but it seemed ok to plant the first seed.

Over coffee, he confided, "Please don't take this wrong because I'm so happy being with you. I got word today that my daughter has cancer and will need surgery and treatment. I'm trying so hard not to bring something negative to our date since it is only the second time we've been together. I'm sorry that I'm not my usual self."

Deanie took his hand, "I'm so sorry to hear the news. You don't have to apologize. You have every right to be worried and distracted."

Wilson didn't go further into the con because it was too soon, but he did like that she was taking the bait.

Outwood

Chapter 18 – Kurt's Car Dilemma

Frustrated, Kurt was speeding to reach the car dealership. As he pulled in, the lights went out. He walked to the door and knocked. At first, no one would come. He shouted, "I know you are in there. I'm staying here all night if needed. I want to talk to someone now."

A man came to the door and said, "Sorry, we are closed."

Kurt said, "Open the door now, Butch."

Butch opened the door but didn't invite Kurt in. "I know you're mad. We warned Mr. Levy about doing the sale. He handled it himself but he's not here right now."

Kurt demanded, "Where is he?"

Butch said, "He takes his wife for drinks and dancing at the Golden Lamb on Fridays. Kurt, don't do anything you will regret. We will get this all straighten out."

Kurt walked into the Golden Lamb. Mr. Levy saw him and hurried over so they could talk outside. "Kurt, I know you said not to do a sale to your wife. That is a new car, but it is just for demonstration. I have your old car on the lot. You and your wife have been such good customers over the years. I could tell that it was important for your wife to have a new car to display at the wedding. She acted like it would be permanent, but I knew better. Just let your wife enjoy the car for the rest of the weekend and bring it back Monday to switch back."

Kurt thanked him. "It actually has caused a lot of problems between me and my wife. At least I don't have to worry about the burden. We are not a charity case and there was nothing wrong with our old car. I will bring it back tomorrow after the wedding. I mean it when I say that there will be no new car for my wife."

Mr. Levy knew the truth about their finances. "Look, I know you like our cars, but we have some good used ones on the lot. Either you can take your car home, or I can sell you a very good car and you can walk away with it and about $5,000.00 in cash. We can

SOCIAL DECEPTION MURDER

discuss it tomorrow." The gentlemen shook hands and the situation was defused.

Instead of going straight home, Kurt drove around the back roads for about an hour thinking of a plan to get their finances straight. He also explored his feelings for Sylvia. He thought about the children who were all adults now.

He concluded that they were going to live within his budget. They were going to save money. He would let her have the nails and hair appointments tomorrow but after that, no more spending until their debt was paid off. If she left him, so be it. He loved his family, but realizes now that he never loved her.

Outwood

Chapter 19 – Taking Control (Saturday)

Kurt woke up early. He went to their bedroom, but Sylvia wasn't there. He called her cell. "The wedding is at noon. I want to leave here at 11:00 at the latest. Where are you and when will you be home?"

Sylvia said, "It's a twenty-minute drive. We don't need to leave until 11:30. I'm at the beauty salon right now. I'm getting my hair done, facial, makeup and nails. I will try to hurry them but I don't know the exact time I will get done."

Kurt became enraged. She had done all that before the dinner last night. More money being wasted. Kurt asked, "What credit card will you be using?"

Sylvia said, "Does it matter?" She listened to the reply, "Ok, I will use the one ending in 9982."

SOCIAL DECEPTION MURDER

As Sylvia enjoyed her pampering, Kurt called all the companies with whom they had credit cards and canceled them. He left two open in case of emergencies but removed Sylvia's ability to charge. He did give approval for a charge from the beauty salon by his wife for today only. He placed a hold on all the credit approval companies so no new charge cards or credit could be given. He doubted if Sylvia had any cards he didn't know about because she had no way to pay them. Their credit was frozen. He had heard on television ads that if you had a certain amount of debt, you could make payment deals with the credit card companies. He planned on Monday to seek out advice on how to do that. There was more interest on their credit cards than the amount they paid each month. They were so indebted he didn't know if they could ever get out of it. He was also considering bankruptcy. He had $500,000.00 in the bank when they married. Now it's all gone and has been replaced with a $50,000.00 debt.

Sylvia's good looks were enhanced to her satisfaction, so she went to pay. She knew the card that she was told to use, but she didn't tell Kurt that she had charged a new dress two days ago to that one. Afraid it would go over the limit, she handed a different card to pay the bill. "I'm sorry, Sylvia, but this card is being declined."

Sylvia was embarrassed and angry, "Well it must be some sort of mistake. They must have messed up our account." She pulled out another card and got the same response. "Kurt told me to use this card." It went through. "I'm going to find out what's going on. My goodness, look at the time. It's almost 11:30. I must run." She went home only to find that Kurt had already left. She switched dresses and hurried to the car.

She called Kurt as she drove. "I'm on my way. I should get there with ten minutes to spare. I need to talk to you. Something is wrong with our credit cards."

Kurt replied, "You should've already been here. It's your son that's getting married. You don't need to make a grand entrance and ruin the day. All the parents that care about him are already here. We will discuss everything after the wedding, not before or during."

Jean was the most nervous of everyone. She was making sure the Pastor had water but warned him not to drink too much because of the ceremony coming up. She did the same for the sound worker. Nick laughed. "Dear, I'm pretty sure they've done this before. Why are you so worked up?"

Jean lifted her finger in the air, "I feel trouble brewing. I'm trying to put out any hot spots before they light up." Jean went in the house to check on Naomi and Violet. As she stepped out of the house to return to the barn, she was hidden from view as Kurt opened the door for Sylvia and could hear her say, "There is something wrong with our credit cards! Two of them aren't working!"

Kurt said, "This is not the time or place for this discussion. We are walking down the aisle to be seated any minute."

"Of course, it is important! Why are you not concerned?"

Kurt answered, "I canceled them. Now act right or I will pull you out of here myself."

They walked in and down the aisle immediately to their seats. Nick and Jean walked down behind them. They also sat in the front row but a few seats away. Nick whispered to Jean, "What is going on?"

She whispered back, "He canceled her credit cards." Nick sat back with a smile on his lips as he watched his son come into the room.

The wedding was so beautiful. When Violet walked into the room, there was a collective sound of happiness. She looked so lovely. Tim was smiling so big that it looked as if his face would break. Everything went perfectly.

The nice thing about barn weddings is that there's no driving afterwards. Pictures were taken of the wedding party quickly to not have the crowd get bored. Alan, with the digital camera, and Fred, with the movie camera. Many in the crowd also had out their cameras and cell phones.

Kurt and Sylvia sat without speaking to each other. Sheriff Taylor, who was the one to introduce Nick and Kurt to law enforcement, sat across from them carrying the conversation with Kurt. Many were helping by removing the food covers and putting in serving spoons. Finally, with pictures done, Tim and Violet led the food line. There was actually a very large crowd of a few hundred people, so the process took a little time.

Glasses of wine or grape drink were being passed out so when Brian stood to give the toast, all were prepared. "I've known Timothy his entire life. I love him like he was my own son. I'm so proud he asked me to be the one to stand here. I'm so happy he found someone so loving as Violet. Nothing is more special than true love. I want give tribute here to my own lovely wife, Anita. Tim, Violet, may your life be as happy and blessed as mine has been."

Naomi stood up, "I don't think Alan and I have had such fun as we do when we hang out with you, Violet and Tim. You bring joy to those around you. I'm glad to say welcome to the family."

The ceremony continued with the couple having their first dance. Sylvia hissed to Kurt, "Jean acted like she was so great yesterday by putting me down when I was critical of the song they chose." Kurt ignored her as usual and continued his conversation with his boss.

Nick and Jean were semi-pros in dancing since it was a hobby that they did a few times a month. They stole the show, which only added to Sylvia ire. The entire crowd danced, talked and enjoyed the great day.

Nick and Jean sat with Brian, Anita, and their daughter, Amber. She received a text and showed great concern. Anita asked, "Is something wrong?"

Amber said, "Before we came here, I got a text from Julie's parents. She didn't come home last night. I told her we all went to Indian Ridge, the same place all the teens have hung out at for generations. I just got a text. They went out there looking around and found her body at the bottom of Ruddy Cliff. Her dad climbed down there and confirmed that she's dead."

Right then, the Sheriff got the message from the office. "I better go. We can leave Libby to handle calls in the office while the rest of my men and I go to the scene."

Nick offered, "Do you want me to come help?"

Sheriff Taylor replied, "No, you and Kurt need to stay here to be with your son. This is too important of a day for him. I'm sure my other deputy and I can handle it just fine."

Outwood

Chapter 20 – The Crime Scene

Tim and Violet were getting their bags to put it in the car. Since it was a rental, Alan and Naomi decorated it with materials that would be easy to clean off and not damage the car. The plan was to stay in the hotel at the airport for the night. In the morning, they would fly to Florida. Alan would make sure the newlyweds were safe at Nick's condo before heading home.

The bride and groom ran to the car with the crowd cheering and colorful balloons flying off into the sky. Alan told Jean, "One week into your marriage and already we have a murder happening. I knew you would end up involved somehow."

SOCIAL DECEPTION MURDER

Jean turned to Nick. "Don't blame me for this one. It happened in your hometown. Do we go back to the hotel or the crime scene?"

Nick stated, "The Sheriff said they didn't need my help. I say let's head back to the hotel." Jean just stared at him. Nick continued to protest, "What? You heard him say our help isn't wanted."

Jean asked, "Has this sheriff ever investigated a murder?"

Nick admitted, "No. There has never been a murder in the history of Outwood. But this is out of my jurisdiction. I have to be invited to intervene."

Jean was stubborn, "I know we don't even know this girl, but I have it in my gut this will end up involving us. I think we should just go by and just look at the scene, even if we don't give any opinions."

Nick relented and they drove to the site of the crime. The police working the scene knew him and greeted him with a welcome except Sheriff Taylor. "I thought I told you we can handle this. You should be at the wedding."

Nick assured him, "The kids are already on their way to their honeymoon suite. Alan and Naomi will be staying at the same hotel and will be flying back home with them. They are happy and well taken care of. I just thought I would drop by and see it for myself. I have no intentions of interfering."

Jean was already walking carefully in approved areas and stooping to looking for things on the ground. Sheriff Taylor growled, "You need to keep her under control. She shouldn't be here. It's no place for a woman to be."

Nick assured him, "She has been to more crime scenes than you. She knows what she is doing." Jean continued examining the trail to where the body was thrown into the gully below. Next, she was in the parking lot, stooping down, getting up, moving and inspecting again.

The Sheriff shouted, "Jean, come back here." When she arrived, he said, "I don't want you walking around mucking up my crime scene."

Angry at his tone of voice, Jean retorted, "Your men already did that for you. I hope you got copies of those tire tracks of the car that was here, then left and came back and parked over there. I hope you have the castings of the footprints that pulled the body to the cliff." Turning to Nick, she asked, "Can you let me know if I'm seeing things correctly? The person that probably did the murder, or at the very least pulled the body, was wearing a size 11 boot with a defective sole, but they had a much smaller foot than the size of the boot." Looking at the Sheriff but pretending to talk to

SOCIAL DECEPTION MURDER

Nick, she continued, "I'm making this statement because of the way the boot did a bend before the place where the toes would be located. It had to be a smaller person pulling because the victim wasn't that large of a woman. I saw them putting her on the stretcher and I would guess she is 5 foot 5 inches, 125 pounds. A bigger man could have carried her instead of dragging her along the ground."

The Sheriff interrupted. "Maybe he didn't want to get blood on his clothes."

Jean argued, "The body wouldn't have been dragged at a lying low position. A stronger man could have not touched the body but pull it up so only the heels would drag. The person dragging the body was small. They had to take a step back, sink in their heels and pull hard time after time to get her to the ledge. I would say that she knew the person because she had been lying against that log over there. There is no indication that she tried to get up or run off. Also, there appears to have been many cars here earlier, so there was probably a group of people with her at one point. The tire tracks I spoke of first parked over there under that tree but then the same tracks are to the left in the soft sand. The boot marks are by that set of tracks but not the other. Whoever drove that car left and came back with boots on. Is that how you read it, Nick?"

Nick said, "I agree with all your points and I can see them from here, but since I wasn't invited to investigate, I can't tell if you missed anything or not."

Jean continued, "When the body was placed on the stretcher, you could tell the rigor mortis was starting to wear off. With it being a cooler night, I would guess the death occurred between 9:30 to midnight."

Sheriff Taylor turned to Nick, "Does she think she is a police detective?"

Jean explained, "I was a crime scene reporter for years. Also, I know how to look and read what is there and not assume."

The Sheriff turned and marched away after saying, "I know who those boots belong to, without the cast." He then gave the order for the casting prints of the boot area and the tire tracks.

Nick told Jean, "At least you got him doing a part of what he should be doing. I'm glad we came. Wait here." Nick did a quick tour of the crime scene performing his own search for clues. In his mind, he was thinking about the boots that needed to be resoled. No one does that anymore. Boots are cheap enough to just get a new pair. He knew this would hit home with the family soon.

Outwood

Chapter 21 – Car Return

When Kurt was ready to leave the wedding, he told Sylvia, "I'm driving the Mercedes to the dealership and you will follow me in the truck."

Sylvia argued, "Why can't we talk about this before we return it?"

Kurt stood firm, "We have no money. There is no way I can pay for this. Even if you were to get a job, it will be minimum wage since you never worked and have no special skills."

"Can't I at least be the one to drive it to the dealership?"

Kurt was very unhappy, "No. It is going back today. I don't trust you to drive it there. Even if you leave me stranded, I can get someone from the dealership to bring me home or call Brian to come get me." He got in the car and drove off.

Marie came out and said, "Thank you and Kurt for helping with the cleanup. It was such a lovely wedding. I couldn't be happier."

Sylvia, not totally an unpleasant person, gave her a hug, "Thank you for all you did on planning the wedding. I'm not sure why, but Timothy clearly didn't want my help or input. I'm sure we will be seeing each other more often now since we are in-laws."

When she arrived at the dealership, Kurt was already inside doing the paperwork. Sylvia slipped in and sat in the chair beside him. She spoke to Mr. Levy, "I'm sorry I caused so much trouble. I thought it would be a pleasant surprise for Kurt."

Mr. Levy knew she was trying to cover the truth, "I told you it was a lender to begin with. If you wanted to surprise Kurt, he's more of a pickup truck type of guy. I was telling your husband about some used cars on the lot that are in really good shape and you could still walk away with money in your pocket. I have no trouble finding buyers for used Mercedes that have been well maintained."

The look on Sylvia's face was like she had just been slapped. Kurt finally answered, "Let us think about that for a day or two, if you don't mind." Sylvia's face showed the sign of relief.

SOCIAL DECEPTION MURDER

When they got home, they sat down for a long talk. Kurt admitted to blocking all the credit cards and freezing their credit. He suggested, "You have clothes with tags still on them upstairs. We will spend NO money except for food that we cook and eat here and pay the electric bill. I'm considering cutting the cable television, but I will keep the internet. I'm very serious. We are broke. I'm going to get help working with the credit card companies so the interest doesn't keep compounding. I will check at work to see if bankruptcy would make me lose my job. I know it does for teachers. I won't rest until we are out of debt and have a savings. You are either with me or I move out and we divorce. With me assuming the debt, your alimony won't be enough to live on."

Sylvia could tell she lost not just the battle but also the war. "Some of my clothes still have the price tags on them. I will find the receipts and return them. There are websites that sells slightly used clothes. You let me keep our car and not trade it in. I will sell what I can. Besides, selling used clothing is now an "in thing" to do. I will look like I'm with the times and not make us look desperate. I will even look for a job. It will occupy my time, so I won't have time to shop."

Kurt kissed her, "I would like for us to work as a team and build a better life together. I just can't live with the debt any longer. We've had a lot of years together and I would prefer to be there for our children and grandchildren together."

"I wonder what kind of job I could do and enjoy? I never considered working before, but I do love houses. Do you think I could work as a realtor?"

Kurt thought, "That is a really good idea because you know all the people in town. You love looking at other people's houses to see their decorations. The only problem is that it costs a few thousand to go to the class, pay for and pass the test, and then you need business cards, signs and things. Why don't you talk to Herbert Guy and see if he will let you work as an assistant at the realtor office? You might try the library and church to see if they have any openings."

Sylvia pretended to be excited about the job hunt but inside she was in total depression. She wanted to be rich and not work at all. Since she couldn't figure out an alternative, she would pretend to go along with the plan for now anyway.

Outwood

Chapter 22 – Visiting Brian

Brian called and invited Nick and Jean over for drinks and snacks. "We built a stone fireplace in the back. Let's sit there, where it will be really relaxing. Anita and I have never met Jean before. There have been so many people around, we've hardly had a chance to visit. I know you leave tomorrow with the grandchildren for a few days and this is our only chance."

Felling guilty, Nick agreed. "I'm really tired. It has been a long day between the wedding and going to the crime scene. We didn't spend much time there, but I'm still wore out. I'm taking a nap, so we will come over in about an hour and a half."

MIA TENROC

Jean said, "You know how I hate to nap. I will go sit in the garden outside and check with Alan to make sure he arrived at the hotel."

Taking advantage of the time alone, Jean called Josephine for a report, "We now have 8 people that have come forward as being cheated. They are all on board with our plan. Having Priscilla put out the warning has caused quite the reaction from Wilson. He is in a panic. I expect him to take action soon. He started his lie about the sick daughter last night, but hasn't requested any money yet. He called Deanie this morning and apologized for ruining the play for her. They are on a picnic now with Gwen and Klaus following a little behind. The pin that Klaus bought works great. They can't talk to her, but they can hear most of what is being said. At least we know she is safe."

Jean told her sister, "Can you believe that Nick thinks we are up to something? He accused me of it but didn't push further. I tried to play innocent but I know I'm not fooling him."

Nick joined Jean in the garden with lemonade about 45 minutes later. "I talked to Alan and they arrived at the hotel with no problem. Tim and Violet are in their room for now, but Naomi and Alan plan to meet up with them for dinner tonight."

SOCIAL DECEPTION MURDER

Nick and Jean arrived at Brian's house at the scheduled time. They went into the backyard where there was a nice fire roaring. "We had leftovers on the s'mores from last night. Beer and wine are at the bar under the awning."

"This is really nice," Nick said. "We talked to Alan and they are all settled at the hotel. This has been a good ending. Amber, you have been really quiet. Are you ok?"

Amber got up to leave, "I'm so sorry but I'm really upset over what happened last night. I'm not very good company. Do you mind if I go to my room for just a little bit? I will be back to visit later."

Brian and Anita looked worried. Jean asked, "Was she good friends with the girl that died?"

Anita confided, "Amber never had fit in with the cool crowd. This girl, Julie, gathered the girls that were somewhat loners to be a part of her crowd. She was a couple of years older and had a lot more experience in life than what Amber has, so I wouldn't say they were good friends, just friendly with one another. Amber was there earlier last night. She said there was a lot of people still there when she left. Amber doesn't handle death well because we lost our son about a year ago. The police said it was suicide, but I feel he was driven to it. I had hoped this visit with you, Jean, would be a happy one. I'm sorry I brought up my son's death, but that's why Amber doesn't handle the loss of people she knew well."

Brian wanted to vent more, "I don't feel that they were good friends because Julie wasn't a nice person and Amber was smart enough to see that. The other kids hung out with her because they were afraid of what she would do or say behind their backs. It was self-preservation. I didn't like Amber running around with her at all."

Nick asked, "Who was this Julie? Do I know her parents?"

"They aren't from around here. They moved into Outwood last October. He was a big shot at the bank. There's a branch in this town. He said he was semi-retired and felt that running an office in a small place like this was the same as being retired. My understanding is that they wanted to get their daughter away from the big city and to experience a simpler life. She was nothing but a pain. According to Kurt, which I believe, he pulled her over for a speeding ticket. She made a pass at him and said she would be willing to work off the ticket another way if he wouldn't write it. He wrote her the ticket anyways, so she reported him to the Sheriff claiming he made the pass at her. Sheriff Taylor actually laughed in her face. He knew it was a lie too. He called her parents, and they arrived and pulled her out of the place apologizing, so they clearly didn't believe her either." Brian then tried to change the subject to something more cheerful. "It's nice to get to know you, Jean. Nick doesn't come up very often. This is your first trip, isn't it?"

Jean noticed a reaction from Nick to the story but since he didn't say anything, she continued to attempt a normal conversation. "Yes, this is my first time visiting Outwood. Nick does pay for the kids and the grandchildren to come visit us in Florida each year. There is so much to do where we live. You should come visit, especially in the winter when it is cold here."

Brian teased, "Not into skiing and ice hockey?"

Nick corrected, "We have great hockey in our state, but we only play it indoors."

"I've always wanted to do some snowmobiling," Jean stated.

Anita pointed to the garage, "We have two machines in there. Come up anytime. Nick, I understand you not wanting to be here, but you know everyone in town loves it when you come."

Suddenly, they heard shouting and sobbing sounds coming from the street. Sylvia was screaming at Sheriff Taylor. "Are you out of your mind? You know Kurt would never do anything like that! What is wrong with you?"

Kurt was getting into the back of the patrol car without saying a word.

Sylvia ran across the street. "Nick, you have to do something! You know Kurt would never kill that girl!"

Nick stood silent. Brian was going over to talk to the Sheriff, but he just pulled away. Nick said, "I just heard the motive. The Sheriff said he knew who boots they were when we looked at the footprints at the crime scene. Kurt told me his boots needed new soles and the ones I saw were distinctive. I saw the Sheriff carrying a gun and since Kurt's weapons are already on file in the office, the ballistics must have matched."

Anita was helping Sylvia back to her house. Jean looked up and could tell that Amber had been watching the scene below. Brian remarked, "This certainly wasn't the evening I expected."

Nick responded, "I think you might need to help your wife calm Sylvia down. We will be going."

Outwood

Chapter 23 – The Grandchildren's Plea (Sunday)

In the car, Jean asked, "Do you think he did it?"

Nick didn't say anything for a while and Jean knew it was his sign that the discussion was off limits for now. By the time they arrived at the Inn, she heard his reply, "I don't know. I don't believe he would be the least bit interest in the young woman. Of course, I never believed he would ever betray me, either." No more was said that night. It was a long day so they just went straight to bed. Jean did notice that he tossed and turned more than usual that night, a sign that he had something on his mind.

The next day, the grandkids were scheduled to arrive for their trip to Minneapolis. Nick's oldest son,

James, had already went home. He would bring his children to join them at the hotel tonight. Sarah and her two girls arrived at the same time as John with his two sons. Each grandchild had their little suitcases, but they looked like they were going to a funeral instead of a few days for fun. The oldest grandson came forward, "Grandpa Nick, I want to go have fun, but how can I be happy knowing Grandpa Kurt might be going to jail?"

The littlest granddaughter ran into Nick's arms. "Please, Grandpa Nick, help him! I understand you are a great detective in the big city. You can do it." All four grandchildren pleaded at the same time.

Nick looked up to this daughter, "Did you put them up to this?"

"No. I went ahead and told them the truth this morning because in a small town like this, word gets around quickly and I thought it would be best if it came from me. I would prefer them to go ahead with the trip to avoid the town gossip."

John added, "I understand if you don't want to help since Kurt and Mom wronged you. I don't believe Kurt did this murder. I've never known him to ever do something bad to anyone else."

Nick was caught in a negative position. If he didn't check into the case, the family would think of him as being spiteful. They would hold it against him if Kurt ended up in jail and he possibly could have prevented it. He wasn't happy when he answered the grandchildren, "I will do this only for you, but I don't know that I can find anything to prove his innocence."

Jean asked, "Do you want me to see if we could extend our stay here in this room?"

Nick requested, "John and Sarah, why don't you take the kids home. I will go to the jail and see if I can talk to Kurt before we figure out what to do. Jean, I suggest that you DON'T come along. You managed to get under the Sheriff's skin yesterday. I think I can get further without you."

Sarah raised an eyebrow. "Why would the Sheriff be mad at Jean? You didn't even sit at the same table yesterday."

Jean admitted, "We went to the crime scene yesterday. That old fool has no clue how to read a site or what to do."

Nick said, "See what I mean? She didn't mince words at his incompetence. Jean, I'm taking the car to drive down to the jail. Please just hang around the hotel until I get back."

Jean decided, "I would rather walk up and down the street, taking in the sites of the town while I have the chance."

Outwood

Chapter 24 – Jean's Investigation Begins

As soon as Nick was out the door, Jean knew exactly where to go. The gossip center of any small town was the Café. She entered knowing it would be almost empty, since it was a Sunday and church service was still going on. She took a seat at the counter. The waitress came over, "Howdy. You are new to town. What can I get you?"

Jean really wasn't hungry but said, "I'll take a piece of that chocolate cream pie. I'm Jean. I'm married to Nick Noble. He's busy with family and I figured this was the place to cheat behind his back and get something sweet."

SOCIAL DECEPTION MURDER

They got a laugh, "Nice to meet you. I'm Lola. Nick and I went to high school at the same time. He was a couple of years older than me. What a hunk you got: good looking, smart, and nice. All the girls were after him. I never did understand what he saw in that stuck-up, fake-acting Sylvia. She sure did him wrong. I was shocked at her and Kurt betraying him. I'm sorry, I should keep my opinions to myself."

Jean assured her, "I enjoy the honesty. I like people to tell it like it is. Can you join me since the place is empty? My treat, of course."

Lola shook her head, "I can stand here and talk to you until someone else comes in. Church doesn't let out for about a half hour, so I'll be glad to keep you company until the crowd arrives."

Jean asked, "Will Nick know who I'm talking about if I tell him that I met an old friend of his?"

"I'm the only Lola in Outwood. I don't know if he thinks of me as an old friend. I was mostly the wall flower standing in the background while he was king of the prom. Has he said anything about Kurt getting arrested last night?"

"Not much. He's at the jail talking to the Sheriff now. Nick and I went to the crime scene and I managed to insult the Sheriff by pointing out things he might have overlooked, so I'm trying to keep a low profile now. Maybe he did spot the clues, but I doubt it with him arresting Kurt. The clues didn't point to a man of his size and strength."

That got a hoot from Lola. "He is a good sheriff, but murder isn't something that happens around here. Are you a detective too?"

Jean smiled. "I was a crime reporter for years. I learned a lot from the real police. Most were nice to me because I never repeated something they said without their approval. Did you know the girl that died?"

"I'll talk since you can keep a secret, but don't tell anyone where you heard it." Jean put a finger to her lips indicating they were sealed. "That girl was nothing but trouble. I heard she came from a big city and got into all kind of mischief. They moved here trying to get her away from that old life. First thing she does when she arrived is go after Scott Surely. He's our football quarterback. Actually, he plays all sports like Nick used to. He dumped the girl he dated for three years to go out with Julie. I can tell you his old girlfriend, Jane, hated her. The school got divided into two camps: those that backed Jane and those that feared Julie enough to not buck her. If you didn't do what Julie wanted, she would spread lies about you. The way I hear it, she used her body to control the men around her. This town was better off before she got here. Julie told a lie to the police that Kurt made a pass at her. There was no way that was true."

SOCIAL DECEPTION MURDER

The church bell rang and people started walking toward the Café. Jean said, "Thank you so much for your honesty. I will keep it a secret that you told me. I don't want you to get in trouble with your boss. I know you have to work now but I wanted to thank you before the crowd comes."

Lola suggested, "You want to hear town gossip? Just sit there quietly and you will hear plenty of it in this place. Another piece of cake?" Jean decided to go with green tea.

As the church crowd came in, two different couples came up to talk to Jean. They had been at the wedding. She joined them at their table. "Nick was busy this morning and told me to entertain myself."

The man responded, "I knew Nick wouldn't let his best friend go to jail for something he didn't do. I can't believe the Sheriff would be so stupid to arrest a good man like Kurt."

The remainder of the table expressed not only innocence for Kurt but added information about the victim. Sheriff Taylor walked in and when he saw Jean in conversation, he came over to the table. "What are you doing here?" he demanded.

Jean held up her cup of tea and responded, "Drinking tea. These are some friends of the family. They were at Timothy's wedding. Nick told me he was busy this morning, so what better place to be than enjoying the pleasure of their company?"

The Sheriff felt Jean was acting rude to him again by that response, so he suggested, "I know who these people are. I heard Nick was just leaving the jail, so I suggest you go meet up with him."

Jean apologized to her new friends, "I'm sorry to leave your company but I feel as if I'm being ordered to leave. I have a feeling Nick and I will be around town this week. Hopefully, we will see you before we go. Please feel free to stop by the Inn if you get a chance."

Outwood

Chapter 25 – Comparing Notes

Nick was sitting on the porch swing, waiting for Jean to return. She walked on the porch and stated, "Either you are starting to work on the murder, or we just had our first fight and I didn't know it."

This was a surprising greeting in Nick's opinion. "What on earth do you mean?"

He slipped over so he and Jean could snuggle on the swing. "I was leaving that local diner on Main St., well kind of ordered out by the Sheriff, and I saw you driving down the street. I stuck my thumb out like I was hitchhiking and you didn't even notice me. Either you were so deep in thought about your interview with Kurt or you didn't want to pick up your wife."

Nick laughed and kissed her on the head. "I'm sure if we had a fight, you would have noticed. I don't like it that sometimes you can read my mind. I guess you want to hear all about my discussion with Kurt." Jean nodded yes so Nick continued, "I don't think he did it. I feel I have to stay to help him. We were very close friends for over 30 years. Yes, I resent him for doing me wrong, but he explained the pressure Sylvia placed on him to marry her. He loves my children and was a good father to them. He always made sure the kids stayed in touch with me and that I could share their day. I realize now that it was a blessing for me to be free from Sylvia and how happy I am to be with you."

Jean interrupted, "Yeah. I know how much better you have it now. Get on with the interview stuff."

Nick held her even closer. "Like I said, I'm sure he didn't do it. It was his shoes, his gun, and he has no alibi for the hours of the murder. The weapon and shoes have been sent to the nearest town with a crime lab, but there isn't any doubt on those facts. They left the party Friday night at 9:00 and got home about 9:30. He attempted to return the car that night so he drove to the dealership, which closed at 10:00. He made it but the employees there couldn't do anything and told him to see the owner, Mr. Levy. He found him at the restaurant around 10:00. The dealership knew Sylvia only wanted the car to impress us of how rich and great she was, which of course didn't work, so they gave her a loaner.

SOCIAL DECEPTION MURDER

Mr. Levy assured Kurt that they would give him their old car back on Monday or whenever he wanted to return the loaner. But Kurt was so mad at Sylvia that instead of going home, he just drove around back roads trying to think of what to do. He contemplated divorce but instead decided to cancel all their credit cards and freeze their finances. That way, Sylvia couldn't blame him for the breakup. Either Sylvia would learn to live within their means, or she would be the one to leave. Right now, he said she agreed to live on his budget, but he doesn't trust her and thinks she is just stalling until she finds another option."

"Back to the case, he leaves his shoes on the back porch when he's not on duty. It is open but covered, so the shoes are safe from the elements but they are left in plain sight. The gun is a spare he kept on the nightstand of the master bedroom. He doesn't remember if the house was locked up when they left. They were in a big fight over the car. He had the house key on his key ring, but he only remembers holding the keys to the new car in his hand when they left. He wouldn't normally worry over leaving the house unlocked because this is a safe town. Many people here don't lock their doors, even at night. With riding back roads, no one saw him so if the murder was between 10:00 and midnight, he had no witnesses after roughly 10:15. He told me all about Julie reporting him as making advances at her. He said she made advances towards him, and that he turned her down flat. No one believed Julie because they knew Kurt wouldn't do that and also, she has a reputation of saying anything about anyone to get her way. Besides, if he would have killed her, he wouldn't have been so stupid as to use his own shoes and gun. The evidence about the person dragging Julie's body to the rim of the gully and throwing it in doesn't fit because Kurt could easily have lifted her. He is definitely being framed."

Jean understood and agreed with Nick. She added, "I heard most of the gossip from the waitress at the diner. She seems to know everyone in Outwood and has no trouble sharing it. Even though I was pumping for information, she pretended she didn't know it, but was glad to spill everything. She really is very smart. She had a crush on you at one time but seemed very happy for us, I mean about our getting married."

Nick smiled, "You must have been talking to Lola. She was a freshman when I was a senior in high school. She has worked at the diner since she was 16. She pretends she doesn't like working there, but she actually loves it because she can get the inside scoop on everyone. Go on, I want to hear what Lola has to say about this."

"She thinks Kurt would never kill Julie. She said if Kurt would kill anyone, it would be Sylvia, and he should get a reward for that, not put in jail. It appears your ex-wife is the town joke and disliked by most

SOCIAL DECEPTION MURDER

people. Anyway, back to Julie. When she first arrived in Outwood, she immediately started putting the moves on Scott Surely, the big man on the high school campus. He's the star of all sports, including being a quarterback on the football team. He has a full scholarship to play football at the University of Nebraska next year. He was dating someone named Jane. She was the head cheerleader and considered part of the in-crowd at school. He dumped her for Julie after dating her for three years. We can add both of them on our list of people to check out. Last week, Julie pulled what the town calls a Sylvia. Julie started sleeping with Scott's best friend, Adam. Now it appears that there is a rift between the two men. I hear that Jane isn't a very nice person either. She's egotistical, selects her friends and looks down on everyone else. I don't think she does bad things to them, but they get hurt when she invites most of the other girls to a party or sleepover and some girls are intentionally not invited. Julie comes into town and dethrones Jane. She gathered those omitted from the cool group and formed her own circle of friends. This consisted of everyone that dislikes Jane. The difference that surfaced after five months is that if you don't go along with Julie's agenda, she will spread gossip about you and try to ruin your reputation. It appears Amber was in the Julie camp. I think we need to interview her, too. I don't know what happened but it appears that two weekends ago, Julie pulled something nasty and most people steered away from her. It was around the time she started sleeping with Adam, though it could've been something else."

Nick decided, "I'm going in and reserving the room for a few more days. I will call the family and let them know that our trip with the grandchildren is off. I will be staying to help Kurt. I know Ken Surely, Scott's grandfather. I will go over to his place and get an interview with Scott through him."

Jean's told Nick her plan, "Julie's last name is Reddick. I will explore on the internet to see if I can find anything about her or her parents."

Nick asked, "Do you know their first names?"

Jean shrugged, "No, but they own a house on Maple, so it won't be hard to check the county appraiser's site to get them. I need to talk to Josephine and Alan and let them know about the murder. I can hear Alan saying something like, 'See Mom, I told you it would happen.' I will let them know that we are keeping it a secret from Timothy and Violet. The kids deserve to enjoy their honeymoon and hopefully this will be cleared up before they return."

Outwood

Chapter 26 – Interview with Scott

Nick kissed Jean goodbye. "I'm off to look up Ken to see if he can get me an interview with Scott. I think it would be better if it were man-to-man. Why don't you stay here and try not to tick off the Sheriff for a change? I might be gone all afternoon but I'll be back in time to take you to dinner."

Nick was surprised at the lack of protest from Jean about not being included. "I have so much computer work to do that I will probably not even leave this room. I want to check in with Alan as well. Don't worry about me, and don't hurry to get back if you're chasing down clues."

Nick had no trouble locating Ken. "Look Ken, I was hoping to talk to your grandson."

MIA TENROC

"No surprise. I thought Sheriff Taylor would come by to talk to him but so far, he hasn't. I can't believe he just locked Kurt up with no investigation." Ken drove Nick to his grandson's house. Scott was shooting hoops in the driveway.

After introductions were made, Nick suggested, "You know I'm a homicide detective, but this isn't official because I'm out of my jurisdiction. I want to ask you some questions. Do you think it would be a good idea to have your parents here?"

The idea didn't appeal to Scott. "I'm willing to talk to you. I don't want to see an innocent person go to jail. What I have to say might be embarrassing, especially in front of my mother. Isn't Grandpa being here good enough?"

Nick assured him it would be. "Rumor has it around town that you dated Julie and broke it off after she slept with your best friend. Is that true?"

Scott smiled, "We call it pulling a Sylvia. No insult to you, of course. That's totally false. Want me to just tell you how it is before you start asking questions?" Nick nodded. "I dated Jane for 3 years. She wanted to wait for sex until marriage. I tried to be understanding. Earlier this year, I realized that I didn't want to spend my life with her. Jane thinks she's better than most people, but she was never malicious to anyone. She basically ignored those that didn't meet her standards.

SOCIAL DECEPTION MURDER

I don't like ego, and I don't feel anyone is superior to another. I've been blessed with talent in sports, a good mind, and women find me attractive, but it's what's inside that matters. Anyways, Julie showed up a few months ago. She acted like she was an independent woman and just wanted to have sex for the fun of it. I tried to do the decent thing and broke up with Jane before going out with Julie. She was really beautiful and desirable. I'm leaving for college soon. With playing football, I have to be on campus by the middle of the summer for practice. I had fun with Julie at first, even though I made sure to use protection, but I began to notice what a cruel person she was. She enacted revenge on anyone that displeased her. She would start hateful rumors, put people down, and tried to think of ways to embarrass people just for fun. I broke up with her about two weeks ago. I told her she could start any rumors she wanted about me because I didn't care. My reputation and my word is good in this town. I told her that she could tell people that she dumped me because she realized that Adam was more fun and a better lover. Adam told me that she was calling and making passes at him, and I just told him to go for it if he wanted to. I explained to him why I didn't want her anymore. Adam was interested in the sex mostly. He never had a really good-looking girl on his arm. He asked if we could still be friends if he went out with her. I said yes but Julie told him to break off our friendship. We still talk on the phone behind her back, but I'm leaving soon anyways so I really don't care what happens. I don't want to throw anyone under the bus, but I think there is a story you might want to check out. There's a meek guy with a great brain at school named Matthew. Julie started putting the moves on Matthew one day, saying she was done with jocks. She arranged to meet him at the campsite we go to. She undressed him, but then she has Adam jump out near naked, flexing his muscles. I guess she then shouted out, 'Who should I sleep with?' and the crowd she runs with jumped out from behind the trees and laughed at Matthew. He grabbed his stuff and ran away crying. I was so angry that I went to him to try to help. I've designated myself as his bodyguard and everyone knows if you mess with him, I will mess with you. I chewed Adam out royally for it. I think he is sorry about the incident but I can't say for sure because he was still infatuated with Julie."

Nick asked, "Do you think Matthew killed her?"

There was silence for a while. "No. He has brains and I told him this would eventually be behind him, even though it wouldn't be easy. I'm not sure if that gave him the hope he needed, though. If you have to talk to him, why don't we ride over to his house together? I don't want him to think I'm telling tales behind his back."

Abletown

Chapter 27 – Second Step of Their Cons

Jean went to their room as soon as Nick left. She called Josephine to see what was happening in Abletown with the con man. "Hi, Jean. Good to hear from you. We are outside of the Driftwood restaurant. Right now, we are on break. Deanie went to the restroom."

Steve jumped in, "Hey there, Jean. This is the best show in town. We are in Fannie's van across from the dining area. We placed chairs in the back of the van and with their cool listening device, we can all hear what they are saying."

Jean asked, "Who all is there?" Each person called out their name. Belinda, Steve, Jake, Klaus, and Josephine. "Who's guarding Deanie?"

MIA TENROC

Josephine explained, "Fannie and our neighbor, Gwen, are inside the restaurant two booths from the door. Deanie is sitting facing them, while Wilson is looking the other direction. That way, Deanie can signal if she needs help. You wouldn't believe what a pain Fannie has been today. We got there to pick her up and she was dressed like a nun. Luckily, Fannie is totally under the spell of Klaus. He was able to explain to her how a nun would appear in public. He selected her clothes, a navy-blue skirt and something that resembles a man's tailored shirt. He found a brown wig and did her makeup. Our usual buxom blonde with a bohemian style is now this subdued, quiet-demeanor woman."

Klaus asked, "Have you ever seen all the bras in her bedroom? One for every day of the month along with every color in a crayon box. They never change their shape. It was like walking along the Gumdrop Forest in the game Candyland." Jean was laughing hard. "I told her that to truly disguise herself, she would need to not stick out like those bras do."

Josephine added, "I lent her one of my bras and then we used a wrap to make her look flat-chested." This sent Jean into great laughter. "We are back live. Deanie just sat down."

Jean could hear Wilson began, "The doctors told my daughter that she had to pay them her co-payment of $500.00 for her to get treatment. I explained to her that most of my money is tied up in investments that I cannot access for the next couple of weeks. Any spare cash I had has already been given to the mechanic repairing the airplane. I don't know what to do. I hate to turn my daughter down when she needs me."

Deanie as Della looked puzzled, "I can't believe the doctors would do that. Can't you put off the work on the plane? Your daughter is more important."

"You're right, she is, but if the plane doesn't get done in time, I will miss delivery of the food shipment to one of the villages. That's very important too, you know."

Deanie suggested, "Why not get a cash advance on a credit card? I know the interest would be a lot, but if you get your investments out in a couple of weeks, you can pay it off immediately."

Wilson was getting upset. He wondered why this woman wouldn't cooperate. He knew the answer, it was too soon to push for money. "You're right. I will look at alternatives for getting the money. Breaking the investments before two weeks would mean a huge loss. I'm sorry to burden you with my problems. We have only been dating a week. This isn't really a matter I should be discussing with you. I just feel so close to you. It seems we have been together a lot longer than that. I respect your opinion, which is the reason I feel comfortable talking to you about this."

Deanie looks lovingly into his eyes. "I feel that closeness to you too. I do hope you continue to confide in me anything that's burdening you."

Wilson asked, "Why don't we go to your house for the afternoon? After dating as often as we have, I feel like I could get to know you better in a less public place."

Deanie tried not to show how repulsed she was. "I have plans with my family today. That is why we are meeting so early. I'm not ready to introduce you to my loved ones yet. Look, I don't mean to be unfeeling about your daughter. I will tell you what I will do. I will pay for lunch. How much money do you have in your wallet? $50.00 is a good amount to work with. Remember when I told you how my husband taught me how to transfer money? I will take your $50.00 and tonight, we will see how much I can make for you. We will meet tomorrow night and I will hopefully have the $500.00 you need. It might be less, it could be more. I have to go study the market first. Do you trust me with that?"

Wilson didn't know what to say. No one ever did this to him before. "Will I at least get my $50.00 back? It would be money toward the $500.00."

SOCIAL DECEPTION MURDER

Deanie snatched the money. "Yes, you will get at least that amount back tomorrow and if I'm successful, you will get much more." She stood up to leave. "Thank you so much for the meal. Well, technically I paid for it so I guess you should be thanking me. I will see you tomorrow. Hopefully if all goes well, the $500.00 won't be a worry for you."

With Deanie in her car returning home, the crowd in the van called her and applauded her performance. Klaus said, "My dear, no one on Earth could have done such a great job. The way you played him left him confused. You were caring and sincere but clear that you aren't giving him your money."

Jake suggested, "Let's meet at the funeral home and discuss scenarios on what he might do next. That way, we can suggest ways to play him at his own game."

Outwood

Chapter 28 – Matthew's Anger

Nick asked Scott, "Is Matthew over 18? If not, his parents need to be with him when we talk."

Scott explained, "Matthew has been 18 since October. I turn 18 a couple of weeks ago. Julie was still 17, which was another reason I needed to break it off with her. Even though it was ok before when we were both 17, she could now get me in trouble because I would be sleeping with a minor. I don't think Matthew wants his parents to know about any of this. There is an ice cream shop by his house. Why don't I call and see if he will meet us there?"

Matthew agreed to meet Scott. Scott failed to mention that Nick was with him. After getting their choice from the ice cream stand that was shaped like a

SOCIAL DECEPTION MURDER

cup of ice cream itself, Scott and Matthew got into the car. Scott introduced Nick.

Nick explained, "I'm not an official policeman here in this state, so you don't have to talk with me. I don't believe Kurt killed Julie. The Sheriff isn't even trying to find out who did it."

Matthew became very anxious, "You told him about me, didn't you, Scott? Now you think I did it. I didn't! She isn't worth destroying my life over, even though the world is a better place with her gone!"

Nick tried to calm the situation first and then asked, "Do you have an alibi? That way, no one can accuse you of anything. I'm trying to find out if you have any ideas on the murder. Do you have any clue who might have done it?"

Matthew continued in an agitated matter, "I was home all night. I was in my bedroom. My parents were downstairs watching television. I can't get in and out of the house without them knowing it. I don't go anywhere now after what happened. She made a total fool of me and now I'm the laughingstock of the town. Scott has been the only one that's been nice to me since then. I'm leaving Outwood at the end of the month. I will come back when I've made a successful life. Not everyone is as cruel as the people in this town. Only two more weeks of school left. I'm not even marching in the graduation ceremony. I'm upset that you would even tell Nick about it, Scott. I thought you were my friend."

Scott sincerely answered, "I am your friend. That's why I told Nick about how cruelly you were treated. He was going to find out anyway from someone, so I thought it was best to be upfront about everything. I told him you were too smart to let Julie ruin your life. I'm your friend and always will be. Just stick close to me the final two weeks and I will deal with anyone saying rude things to you."

Matthew faced Nick and ranted, "Everyone in town hated Julie. The only people who hung out with her were those that feared what she would've done to them if they didn't. I don't know anything else. I was only around her at school and that ... that one night. Hey, why don't you go ask Amber or Nancy? I know they were still running around with her before she died. I've got nothing else to add! I'm going home!" They watched Matthew storm down the street and into his house.

Nick and Scott were talking when there was a knock on his window. "That's Matthew's mother and father," Scott said. Nick rolled down the window.

The mother yelled, "I don't know you, but leave my son alone. He was home on the night of the murder." In a much lower voice, she said, "He doesn't know that we've already heard the gossip about what happened. We don't tell him because he can feel comfortable in his own home with keeping the lie."

The father said, "That girl got what she deserved. We didn't do it and neither did Matthew, but we are all glad she is gone."

Outwood

Chapter 29 – Reporting on Sunday's Investigations

It was late when Nick arrived back at the room. "I brought my favorite pizza for our dinner. Hope you don't mind but I'm not really in the mood to eat out. I'm wanting some time alone with you for a change. Besides, Sunday night is family dinner night for most people in Outwood, so the majority of the restaurants here close by 6:00. Hope you didn't get too bored being left alone."

Jean assured him that she was very busy and asked about his findings.

"Scott, I would say definitely didn't do it. He broke up with her, not the other way around. He saw her for the devious person she was. She was still 17 and when he turned 18, he knew not to sleep with her anymore." Nick then told the story of Matthew. Jean felt so bad for him. Nick expressed his opinion, "I don't think Matthew will ever get over what happened to him. I don't think his parents will either. Both Matthew and his mother fit the size and description that we know the killer had due to the footprints. I think either one of them would have done it. They are both very angry and their alibi is each other."

Jean asked, "I know that anyone had access to Kurt's shoes, but did they have a way to get to Kurt's gun?"

Nick cringed at the thought but suggested, "I think I need to look at that lock on Kurt's house. I need to see how hard they are to pick and if anyone has tried. I want you to come with me and run interference with Sylvia."

Jean laughed, "She hates me. I assure you that she won't talk to me."

Nick gave her a kiss. "To know you is to love you. She felt like you were competition, but now you would be allies. We need to know who had access to the gun."

Jean chewed her pizza very slowly. "Maybe if I take long enough to eat, you will go without me." Her plan didn't work. Nick waited patiently until she was done. They got into the car and started the drive over. "We need to interview Amber as well. Julie's parents were texting her. She could tell us who was there and if anything special happened that night. She also might be able to let us know who 'GoGirl' is."

Nick looked at Jean like she was crazy, "Please explain."

Jean smiled. Her afternoon wasn't wasted, "I've been looking through the public records again. I went on #MeToo to see if anyone else put something on Kurt. There had been two around the time of Julie's false accusation. One was put up but then withdrawn, but the other one stayed on. I tried to research Julie but surprisingly, there was nothing on her. I got her parents name off the address of the house, and the name of the bank he worked for, and found out some interesting information about them. Mr. Reddick was from the Midwest. He worked his way up to regional Vice President of the bank in Indiana. He then moved to Boston about ten years ago after receiving a promotion. He was the guy that the regional Vice Presidents across the country reported to. He got divorced around that time and his ex-wife moved back to Indiana. He married his secretary, of course, who was half his age. She is the current wife. It's never been stated why he stepped down, but they called it a semi-retirement. He isn't 65 yet but he chose to move here and take a much lower position than what he's held for years."

SOCIAL DECEPTION MURDER

They arrived at the house. Nick walked across the street to Brian's and asked him to join in on the house inspection. Sylvia ran out of the house as soon as the car pulled up. "Is there any word about Kurt? Can I go see him?"

Nick responded, "I believe you can see him, but you'll need to call Sheriff Taylor to confirm. We are here for two reasons. First, Brian and I are going to inspect the locks to see how easy it is to get in. Second, we need to go over the list of people that has access to the house."

While Nick and Brian were looking at the house. Jean and Sylvia stood close by. Jean began the questioning and took notes. "Who has keys to the house?"

Sylvia's replied, "Kurt, myself, all four of my kids, and of course, Brian. We look in on each other's house when the other is on vacation. Plus, we do things for each other, like if for some reason Brian and Anita can't get home, they'll call me and I will let their dogs out and feed them. They do the same for Kurt and I. Kurt worries about his hunting dogs when we are gone. My parents and Kurt's parents had a key but when they all passed, we got the keys back. Those keys are currently in the house."

MIA TENROC

As they walked to the back door and looked over that lock, Jean asked, "Do you remember if the doors were all locked on Friday night?"

Sylvia thought, "I'm sure they were. Let me think. Kurt dropped me off at the front door. I had to use my key to get in. I'm sure of that. As for the back door, I didn't try it that night, but I remember it was locked in the morning for sure. I was taking out the garbage after making my breakfast. I can't stand having trash in the house so instead of a big can, I use a little rack that you put grocery bags in, which fill up fast. I opened the door with the key that is kept beside the door. I'm sure of that, so I would say the house was locked up all night. You can ask Kurt, but I believe when he returned, he came in the front door because the driveway was blocked by his truck. When he comes home from work, he always enters through the back door, but I'm sure I heard the front door open that night when he came home."

Nick then questioned, "You didn't go out to the back porch after you returned to check on the dogs or anything?"

Sylvia was certain, "No. I went straight upstairs and didn't come down again until morning."

Kurt and Nick had walked around the house and inspected the windows. Sylvia then questioned, "What are you looking for?"

SOCIAL DECEPTION MURDER

Nick explained, "Anyone could've grabbed the boots even though the dogs would have barked loudly from the kennel. The gun is another matter. I can't find any marks that indicates that the locks were picked. They are good, solid locks so it couldn't have been jimmied to come open. I don't see anywhere else where a window could be pried opened. If the house was locked, then the person who obtained the gun has a key."

Sylvia said to Nick and Jean both, "I can't thank you both enough for trying to help Kurt." She had tears flowing now. "I would understand if you didn't help, but I'm so very grateful you are."

Jean gave her a hug, "Don't worry. Nick is the best. If the answer is out there, he will find it. Just one question, do you know if the four children keep their key to your house on their keyring, or do they have it hanging in the house where anyone can have access?"

Sylvia replied, "All three boys have it on their keyring. My daughter has it in her kitchen because they live really close and the grandchildren often walk over to visit without them. They will carry the key with them."

Nick turned to Brian, "We really need to talk with Amber. With the text she was receiving, I assume she was with Julie Friday night. We need to know who else was there and if anything special happened."

Brian shook his head, "Sorry, but Amber is so upset over this whole thing that she wanted to get away. Since tests and school activities are for the most part done for the students at school, we thought it was best for her to get away. Anita took Amber to her mother's house. They were going to shop and go to a movie just to hang out."

Outwood

Chapter 30 – Interrogating Joy (Monday)

Back at the hotel, Nick explained, "Brian's son, Victor, was very smart and wanted a life in a big city. He didn't like the little town and wanted to live where he could have new people and experiences in his life each day. He moved to Boston after law school and landed a very good job at a prestigious firm. He was out at a bar one night and met this beautiful young woman. When the waiter carded the girl, he sold her drinks. She said she was 23 but in reality, she was only 16. She looked older than her age. Victor found out the hard way that she lied. The police arrested him for having sex with a minor. Her mother filed the complaint. The law firm fired him because he brought a bad name to the firm. They claimed so many people saw him being taken out in handcuff that it resulted in a loss of business. The girl then posted on #MeToo how Victor always knew she was a minor and yet forced himself onto her. She claimed she never had a fake id. The waiter couldn't remember for sure if she was the one he carded that night. Victor became despondent. His license to practice law was revoked. The thought of jail time was more than he could take. He took his own life one night. The whole family was torn apart. Amber worshipped her older brother and hasn't gotten over it. I think that is why she is having such a bad reaction to Julie's death."

Jean got the information on Victor and was on the computer. "The case is sealed because of a minor being involved." She looked up news articles and again struck out on finding much information. "Nick, can you call Brian and find out if he knows the name of the girl in the case and also if he knows who this GoGirl might be?"

"It's kind of late tonight. Why don't we tackle it tomorrow? I plan to talk to Kurt again to see if he could think of who had access to the gun. He might know the answer to that question. Brian is very touchy about the subject."

The next morning, Jean was up and ready to go. Nick dropped her off at the diner on his way to the jail.

SOCIAL DECEPTION MURDER

"I think Sheriff Taylor still doesn't welcome your company."

Getting out of the car, Jean retorted, "I guess he can't stand someone that knows more than he does."

Inside, Lola welcomed her. "I had a hunch that you would come in today."

Jean explained, "Nick's out hunting down clues. By any chance do you know someone that uses GoGirl as her email?"

Lola laughed, "You think I'm the town gossip center?"

Jean assured her, "I think you are in the best position to listen in Outwood. I live in a small town too, you know. Even if the diner isn't a gossip center, it is the town meeting hub."

"Meeting hub, I like that term better. GoGirl is actually the biggest nerd in town. Here is her name and address. She should be in school today, though."

Jean pressed, "Do you know if she is under 18 or not?"

Lola was impressed, "I'm afraid that I don't know that, but her mother works from home and is there all day. You could ask her first."

Jean ordered breakfast and Lola talked to her as much as she could. When leaving, there was another large tip for Lola in appreciation of her time. "You could easily be a detective, Lola. You know more about reading people than most. You also know what the conversation is about without it being expressed into words."

Jean texted Nick the address where she was going to. She only told Nick that she was checking on a clue. When the door was answered, Jean explained "Mrs. Peterson, I'm Jean Noble. My husband…"

Mrs. Peterson quickly interrupted, "I know who your husband is. He's a little older than I am. I was in grade school when he was the star quarterback, hockey player, and all-around athlete. In a small town like this, there is nothing else to do. Everyone goes to the school sporting events, so I know who your husband is. Why are you here?"

Jean explained, "We don't think Kurt killed Julie, yet the Sheriff has him in jail for it. We don't feel the case is being thoroughly investigated. Well, to be fair, since the Sheriff has never dealt with a murder investigation before, I don't think he understands the clues. Nick and I are trying to help Kurt. Do you think he did it?"

Mrs. Peterson invited Jean in to sit. "I don't think he did it. I don't have much time because I'm working even though I am at home. Can you be more direct about what you want?"

SOCIAL DECEPTION MURDER

Jean responded, "Your daughter posted a #MeToo entry saying that Kurt harassed her at a traffic stop. Was that true?"

"What? No, that wasn't true. I don't think that my daughter has ever interacted with Kurt."

"I understand you are busy, Mrs. Peterson, but this is extremely important. Can we go ask your daughter about it?

Mrs. Peterson was putting her computer on sleep and grabbing her purse. "Let's go to the school. I don't want my daughter getting into trouble. I want to be there when you talk to her. I also want to find out if what you are saying is true. My daughter better not have made any false statements to get someone in trouble."

At the school office, Jean and Mrs. Peterson was shown into an empty office space while the receptionist called for Joy Peterson to join her mother. The girl came in looking very scared, "Why are you here, Mother?"

Mrs. Peterson didn't beat around the bush with her daughter, "Did you do this posting that accuses Officer Kurt of harassing you?"

Joy blushed, "I didn't, but it was posted from my phone. Julie's family never let her use the computer without them being present. They wouldn't let her have internet on her phone. Whenever she wanted to go online, she would borrow my phone. She did the posting from a couple of different phones. I didn't know how to take it down so I just hoped it would never become an issue."

Mrs. Peterson was so mad she threatened, "I will talk to your father but as far as I'm concern, you might lose your internet privileges as well."

Jean jumped in using a calm voice, "Joy, were you with the group at the campfire the night Julie was killed?"

Looking at her mother before answering, she knew to tell the truth, "Yes. There were only 8 of us. The group used to be bigger, but a lot of families no longer let their kids hang out with Julie. Besides her, there was Adam, Tom, Andy, Amber, Glenda, Nancy and me. Adam was trying hard to put the moves on Julie and encouraged the remainder of us to start making out with each other. Julie got irritated and asked him to leave. The three guys took off. Julie started bragging about all the men she had slept with. She didn't mention who they were exactly, but she said that after sleeping with some big important men in Boston, that sleeping with a country bumpkin was so uninspiring. I was surprised when she mentioned Boston. She then went on a rant about her parents, how they controlled her life and that they forced her to change her name. I

SOCIAL DECEPTION MURDER

know she and her stepfather didn't like each other at all. She said once before that she threw up in her mouth every time she had to say her last name was Reddick. Anyways, Julie kept chatting away, but to be honest, I really don't remember much of what else she said. She liked talking about herself and, well, I don't know, but I think she lies a lot. After a while, Amber got upset and said she had to leave."

Jean was eager for more information but tried to appear calm. "Did Julie have a car? Did she leave when you did?"

Joy sensed what she was saying was important. "No, she didn't. Nancy, Glenda and I stayed with her for another fifteen minutes, but we mostly just talked. It was getting cold and really boring. Julie then ordered us to leave. We invited her to ride home with us, but she said she wanted to be alone for a while, so we just left."

Jean didn't like where this was going but was sure she now knew the truth.

Outwood

Chapter 31 – Changing Names

Jean went back to their room. She was glad that Nick declined staying at Brian's house. A text came in from Nick. He was going to the school to see if he could get an interview with Adam. He said it was best to talk man-to-man again, which was his way of saying that Jean wasn't invited. Nick was nice enough to phrase it that he felt Adam would talk more in private without a woman around.

Jean was relieved. She sat down at her computer to search for more information on the Reddicks, starting with a wedding date. She searched news and social articles as well as trying to access the county records regarding marriages. It appeared that Mr. Reddick married his secretary just over 2 years ago. She could find no details on the wedding. It appears to have just been done at the courthouse with the Justice of Peace signing off after residing over the ceremony. This was only a couple of months before the charges against Victor. Mr. Reddick was named Raymond. He married Janet Morrow. Jean then went to the census rolls. The last one listed Raymond with wife, Janet, and stepdaughter, Meredith, 16.

Jean called Sarah, since she taught at the elementary school. "Do you know anyone at the high school that could look up some records for me?"

Sarah offered, "I do, but information on a student is confidential and while they will give it to me, they might not give it to you. What do you need?"

Jean requested, "I need to have you check the school transfer records to see if Julie Reddick ever went by another name."

Sarah asked, "How important is this? I can have the student teacher lead the class if you need it right now. If not, I will look it over after school is out." Jean left that up to Sarah. "Is this a clue that could get my dad out of jail?"

Jean just stated, "It could be very important, but it's not like your dad is going away right now, so it's not an emergency."

MIA TENROC

Jean continued her computer work when, under a half-hour later, Sarah called back. "Jean, you're not going to believe this."

Jean stated, "That Julie Reddick is also known as Meredith Morrow?"

Sarah was quiet for a minute. "You already knew, didn't you?"

"I was pretty sure."

Sarah was searching for words again, "Do you know the story of Brian and Anita's son, Victor? This is the same name and age as the girl that caused his death. Oh my gosh! Amber was alone that evening. They have a key to our house, so she could have had access to the gun and boots. Please tell me I'm wrong. Amber is such a wonderful person that I've known for my whole life. She would never do something like this. Does Nick know this information?"

Jean sounded firm, "Sarah, please listen to me. I will handle this. It will tear Nick apart to have this information. Please trust me. I will let him know at the right time. I have another plan for now. Again, please don't say anything to anyone else right now. It is best to go through the proper channels and not involve your father, Nick, that is. I'm glad to see you inherited part of his genius that has reasonable deduction."

Outwood

Chapter 32 – Sheriff Taylor and Raymond Reddick

Jean marched into the police station and asked for Sheriff Taylor. He was not happy to see her, "What do you want?"

Jean replied, "To speak in private."

Afraid of what she might do or say, he took her into the office and shut the door. "Why do I get the feeling that Nick doesn't know you are here?"

Jean looked him straight in the eye, "Do you really believe that Kurt did this?"

The Sheriff looked very uncomfortable. "No. I would never believe he did it, but it was his gun and boots. He has no alibi and he has a motive due to a complaint Julie placed against him a few months ago. What am I supposed to do, ignore the clues?"

Jean started with, "Nick can't be the one to solve this. He loves Amber, as well as Brian and Anita. This is your county and your responsibility. I'm giving you what information I have and am willing to do more work if you need it, but this needs to come out through your department and from you. I found out that Julie Reddick had a name change. She was originally known as Meredith Morrow." The Sheriff froze. The pen he had in his hand dropped onto the desk. He knew the name. "I don't want to believe this but Amber, Joy, Glenda, and Nancy were with Julie that Friday at the campfire site. Joy just told me about Julie ordering the three man that were there to leave. She started bragging about the rich city men she had affairs with." The Sheriff put his head into his hands as Jean continued, "Amber had the key to Kurt's house. She had access to the gun and boots. She knew the four adults were at the rehearsal dinner for Timothy. Remember how I stressed the two tire prints at the crime scene? I can't swear to it but I'm pretty sure that they match the tires on Anita's car. I looked when I was there the other night. Remember when we talked about the boot prints? A smaller foot than Kurt was in them because of the way the toes bent when walking. The draw marks of the body showed that someone smaller was trying to

SOCIAL DECEPTION MURDER

drag it. It all fits." There was a long silence before she asked, "What do you plan to do with this information?"

Sheriff Taylor got up and said, "Let's go."

Jean asked, "Where? Amber is with Anita, and they are out of town right now."

The Sheriff growled, "To the Reddick house!"

The Reddick couple seemed surprised with the visit. Janet asked, "I thought you had the person that killed our daughter in jail. What could we possibly do for you?"

Sheriff Taylor began, "Did you, for the benefit of your daughter, press charges against Victor Johnson in Boston last year?"

Stunned, Janet responded, "Well, yes, but what does that have to do with our daughter's death?"

Mr. Reddick looked ready to explode but said nothing. Sheriff Taylor shouted, "Then why in the hell did you move to his hometown? Did you come to rub salt in the wounds of those that loved him?"

Raymond spoke calmly, "We didn't know that Victor originally came from here until just now. The situation with Victor took place in Boston, and his listed address was in Boston." He turned to his wife and stated, "She destroyed my life and everyone else's life that she ever associated with. We are better off with her gone." Janet began to cry. To Jean and the Sheriff, he continued, "I married Janet about two years ago. I left a long, successful marriage. Like so many men when they have their midlife crisis, I strayed. Janet was exciting and beautiful. I had no clue about the baggage that came with her in the form of Meredith. She probably has told lies a dozen times on #MeToo about good people that didn't deserve it. Against my wishes, Janet forced the issue about prosecuting Victor Johnson. If he would have fought, he could've proved that she did things like this to other people, but he didn't fight. I was shocked when he committed suicide. The bank couldn't take all the bad publicity that might've happened. They transferred me here and told me to get the girl under control or that I would be fired. We changed her name and restricted her use of the internet. We even came to the police station when Julie filed the complaint against the officer and declined to press charges because we knew it was another one of her lies. I don't know what else we could have done."

Jean said, "She still was posting lies. She just borrowed her friends' phones to do so. The sick thing about all this is that those who truly have been abused are discredited by the fakes. It's unbelievable that this was the location the bank transferred you to."

Raymond continued, "It was the smallest, most remote place to put me. I went from making major money in a prestigious position to entry level management, and it was all for nothing." He turned to his wife, "You knew nothing about parenting. You supported her in her wrong and wicked actions. Instead of coming down on her, you went after those she had hurt." Janet got up and ran to the bedroom. "What do you want us to do now? Do you think someone related to Victor murdered Meredith? If so, I won't press charges and neither will she. I guarantee that."

Sheriff Taylor angrily replied, "I wish it was that easy. This was murder. I feel it was justified but still, the law requires that the person who did it needs to pay for their crime."

Sheriff Taylor and Jean left. In the car, he asked, "Did you walk to the station?" Jean nodded yes. He drove her to where she was staying, "I'm not going to believe right away that Amber is guilty even though there are a lot of things pointing in that direction. I appreciate you giving me the information you gathered. I know now that I will need to interview all the people that were there that night. I wish I could forget it. Don't say anything to anyone. Give me your phone number in case I want to get hold of you. You are really good at getting information out of people. What's your secret?"

Jean smiled, "Listening and steering the conversation to the topic you want them to talk about. Let them do all the speaking and if they stop, just ask a probing question. It doesn't work on everyone, but it's usually effective with people that want to get something off their chest. Besides, if you lead the conversation, they might answer your questions ask but you might miss out on vital information you wouldn't know to ask about."

Abletown

Chapter 33 – The First Delivery

Jean couldn't wait to get back to the room. She hoped Nick wouldn't be there for a while. It was 1:00. Josephine had texted that Deanie was about to meet with Wilson.

Abletown was so small that even though she wasn't there that often, Deanie feared that someone might still recognize her. Therefore, she selected an inexpensive sandwich shop near the shopping district in the nearby city for this date. Again, she chose somewhere with outdoor dining. The team was in Fannie's van with the listening device in place.

Fannie complained, "While the show is good, I don't get to dress up and be in it."

"Quiet! Here they come with the food," said Belinda.

As soon as they were seated, Deanie reached into her purse. "I managed to turn your $50.00 into $552.00. I took out the cost of our last dinner, so here is $516.00, just enough for you to send off to your daughter today. Hopefully the doctors will deal more honestly with her. I've never heard of a doctor requiring an upfront payment. Usually, they get so much off the insurance company that they waive their personal co-pay."

Wilson looked overjoyed. "Della, I can't thank you enough. You don't know how much this means to me. I wish you would teach me your money trick."

Deanie shook her head, "No. I won't do that. It's my secret. Anyways, I chose this place because it's very nice but not expensive. Maybe we can find other ways to enjoy our time together that doesn't include spending money on expensive restaurants or tickets to plays. Tomorrow is Tuesday, and the gardens are open to the public. We can walk around and see the flowers. The roses are about to come in bloom."

Wilson reached out and took her hand. "Let's make that a date for tomorrow. Is noon good for you?" He lifted the hand to kiss it.

Deanie giggled like a young girl. Instead of getting upset, Klaus said, "Well played, girl. I know she is really repulsed by him, but you would never know it. That's why she is an award-winning actress."

Deanie continued, "Do you like our being together every day? I'm not becoming too much for you, am I?"

Wilson slid his chair around so they were side-by-side instead of across the table. "I can't get enough of you. I wish we could be together more often. Instead of the plays, we could always get a copy of a movie you like, and I can bring the popcorn. We could curl up at your place and spend some time alone together." No response from Deanie, so he asked, "You got together with your family last night. How did that go?"

Deanie immediately went into a story of the meal and the members of the family that were there. Finally, she decided on her lie. "Wilson, I haven't been totally honest with you about something. My youngest daughter and her two children moved in with me about a month ago. It's only temporary. My daughter lost her job a few months back. She has found another one and is getting paid well. It should only be a few months before she saves enough to get a place of her own. She plans to stay close by so the grandchildren can stay in the same school and come to my house afterwards so they won't be alone. Their care and attention usually take up my time between 3:15 to about 5:30. That's the reason why I wanted to meet early today and my suggestion for tomorrow. I'm free in the evenings but until I'm more sure about our compatibility, I'm not ready to introduce you to my family. I hope you understand. It has been a wonderful 10 days together, but that still is a short amount of time."

Wilson honestly said, "I agree. I'm not ready for our families to meet yet either. I appreciate your honesty. Do you really think this is temporary? A lot of multigenerational families live in the same house these days."

He still hugged Deanie and rubbed her shoulders and neck. Deanie hated when he did that but pretended to like it. "I just can't believe how much we have in common with our taste in music and interests." After about an hour of boring chatter, she looked at her watch. "Oh my, look at the time. I need to get on the road so I'm home on time. I will meet you at the gardens at noon tomorrow. Do you need directions?" After providing the information, Deanie got in the car and left.

Klaus turned to Belinda, "Thanks for lending Deanie your Mercedes. I hope him knowing the make and model doesn't create a problem for you if he tries to track her down."

Outwood

Chapter 34 – Temporary Release

Back at the police station, Sheriff Taylor had his deputy brought into his office. "Kurt, I really don't believe you committed the murder. I've known you your whole life. You are a good and reputable man. I talked with the DA and the Judge that will handle this case when it comes to trial. We agreed that you should be out with no bond. I'm exploring other avenues, but none of them look like a happy ending for someone in Outwood, and for the town as a whole. We are a very close community and what hurts one of us hurts all of us. I have to ask you to stay available and not leave the county. Do you agree to those terms?"

"Can I have my job back?"

MIA TENROC

"Sorry, Kurt, not until you've been cleared. Most of the townspeople are behind you, so maybe we can find someone to give you a job temporarily. I can't have you be a part of the investigation team, but I will tell you that Raymond Reddick doesn't even want me to find the killer."

"I'm kind of hurt that you even arrested me to begin with. I know the evidence made me look bad, but you know me. You knew I would never do anything like murdering a teenager. Maybe getting a job somewhere else would be the best thing. I'm good at auto repair. I've kept my old truck running for fifteen years now. I think I will go see if I can get on at Bailey's Auto and Body. Bailey and I have been friends for years."

The Sheriff got up, "Let me take you home. If there's anything that I can do, like give a reference or recommendation, contact me. I'm really sorry all this is happening. I'm afraid the gun and boots need to stay here. I feel it is best if I hold all of your other guns for you, too."

When they arrived at the house, Nick was outside with Brian. Brian shook Kurt's hand. "So very good to see you. Are you home for good?"

"I've been released without bail for now. I'm going to look for other employment so if you hear

SOCIAL DECEPTION MURDER

anything, let me know. I live paycheck to paycheck, so I need something quick."

Nick stared at Sheriff Taylor, "Why the change of heart? Do you know who did it?"

The Sheriff avoided the question. He instead replied, "Kurt, I want to take a look at the locks and the entrance of your house to see if anyone got in to get your gun."

Nick seldom got angry, but his tone of voice showed what he felt inside, "Brian and I already did that. There are no signs of anyone breaking into the house or picking the locks. You didn't answer my question. Why the change of heart?"

The Sheriff looked guilty. "Let's just say someone presented me with some incredible evidence that opened up other possibilities. I have to explore all leads. There was no need for Kurt to sit in jail while the investigation continued. Brian, I really need to talk to your daughter. I know she was with the group at the campfire that night. I'm interviewing all the people that were there. She is a very smart girl and might hold valuable clues to help. I understand she is out of town. When do you think she will be available?"

Brian was a little taken back. "Amber is very upset right now. She is at her grandparents with my wife. Can you talk to her over the phone?"

"I would prefer not. It is always better to talk face-to-face. I understand she is upset, but Kurt's life depends on me finding the truth. Can't you persuade her to come home? It would be better for her to visit me voluntarily instead of me insisting."

Brian agreed to try to talk them into coming home.

The Sheriff was getting into his car with Nick following him to it. Nick leaned in, "What information? From whom?"

Sheriff Taylor didn't answer his question but he did reply, "You married well."

Outwood

Chapter 35 – Nick's Questioning

Nick arrived right after Jean listened in on the drama. Jean quickly said, "Nice talking to you, Josephine. We can check in tomorrow about noon again." She turned to Nick and asked, "Hi honey, how is the investigation going?"

Nick didn't look too pleased, "I was about to ask you the same thing. I was at Brian's when Kurt came home from jail. He was told to just stay in town, and that he can't go back to police work yet. No one is telling him or I what's going on, but I got a hint that you were in Sheriff Taylor's office recently."

Jean tried to look innocent. "Why would you think that?"

MIA TENROC

"Ok, let's try it this way. When did Sheriff Taylor change his mind about you? I was there this morning and he was glad you didn't come along. Now he's telling Kurt and I that he misjudged you. If you found something out, why didn't you come to me to discuss what you've uncovered? I'm upset that you went behind my back right now, and I would like to know why."

Jean turned and said sincerely, "No. You don't want to know what I found out. I don't want to place you in a position of compromise. You would need to choose between the people you love. I wish you would trust me on this."

"No! I'm a professional detective. I don't need you deciding what I should know and what I shouldn't. I thought we were a team, but apparently not now."

Jean tried to explain. "This isn't our, or I guess I should say, your territory. The Sheriff is the one that needs to handle the investigation, even if he needed a little push in the right direction. He will be the one to make an arrest if there is one. So far, only he and I are following this line of investigation. Mr. Reddick wants him to turn a blind eye to the case and told the Sheriff that he wouldn't file charges against this person. However, the Sheriff informed him that it was up to the state on a murder case, not him. Mr. Reddick is right now contacting the bank and asking to be relocated as soon as possible. I'm pretty sure he will divorce his wife as well. Can you please know that I would never do anything to hurt you? If I tell you right now what I found out, you WILL be very hurt."

Nick got up and left without a word. Jean texted him, "Please let me know if you will be back soon." No response.

Nick walked to his daughter's house. He was so mad at Jean that he didn't want to be with her. Maybe time with the grandkids would help. Sarah greeted him. "I'm so glad to see you, Dad. Mom just called and said Kurt was home. He's not in the clear, but at least he's not in jail. I guess I have you to thank for that. What happened?"

Nick asked if the grandchildren wanted to throw the ball in the backyard. After a nice time laughing and playing with the kids, Sarah brought out lemonade for them to drink. Nick said, "I don't know what happened. My wife discovered something about the case but she refuses to tell me what it is. In over five years, we've never had a fight. Believe it or not, we've never had an angry moment, even when she was a suspect in her daughter-in-law's murder."

Sarah's eyes went wide, "Five years is a long time to get along so well."

MIA TENROC

Nick grumbled, "Jean claims that I'll be hurt if I found out. I'm a homicide detective, for gosh sakes. I don't need protecting."

Sarah didn't know what to say. She placed a hand on her father's arm. "I think Jean is wonderful, and that she's doing the right thing about not telling you."

Nick turned in surprise, "Why? Did she reveal something to you?"

Sarah smiled, "No, Dad. I'm my father's daughter. You are a great detective. Jean told me that I inherited part of your intelligence. I don't know for sure, but I'm making a guess on who did it and if I'm right, then I truly think that she's making the right call in not telling you."

Total frustration took over Nick. "So both of you think that you know what is best for me?"

Sarah realized the mistake she just made. "Look, I don't want you to be mad at Jean. She doesn't deserve it. You made the correct choice marrying her. Please don't let the anger ruin anything. When it all comes together, you will know we are right."

"Just tell me the part you both know, please. It's important."

Sarah relented, "Julie Reddick isn't her real name."

Nick asked, "When do you think she'll tell me more details?"

"My guess is tomorrow."

Nick went back to the hotel. Jean looked worried, "I love you. I just feel if you weren't so close to the situation, that you would be following the same line of thinking that I am. If I tell you now, you'll have to wrestle with the same dilemma as the Sheriff. It's his burden to carry, not yours."

Nick hugged and kissed her, "I can tell this whole thing is weighing heavy on you right now. Sarah told me to give you one more day. I trust you, but if something doesn't happen tomorrow, will you agree to tell me?" Jean agreed.

Outwood

Chapter 36 – Another Day of Mystery (Tuesday)

Nick awoke to Jean working on the computer some more. "What are you searching now? I thought you spent time there all day yesterday."

Jean motioned him over, "I decided to look up Scott on #MeToo. It seems there were a few postings put up last Wednesday and Thursday about him trying to force himself on a couple of the high school girls in town. This certainly doesn't match what you told me about him. I guess letting Julie say she broke up with him wasn't enough to satisfy her. That doesn't give him motive, and his size doesn't fit the boot marks."

Nick yawned and stretched, "Why do people have to be evil and do bad things? Julie seems to have been

SOCIAL DECEPTION MURDER

a real mental case. She loved destroying others. It's a shame her family didn't get her the psychological help she needed."

Jean accidentally said, "Her stepfather knew it, but her mother thinks she did a fine job raising Julie and that Julie would grow out of it."

Nick's eyebrow went up. "I take it you talked to both of them?"

Jean was trying to think how to back out of this one, "Of course. They are directly related to the murder victim. Why wouldn't I interview them?"

"The Sheriff told Kurt yesterday that Mr. Reddick doesn't want to prosecute the party that did it. Did you hear him say the same thing?"

Jean turned to face her husband. "Yes, the Sheriff and I heard the same thing. This is a case in his jurisdiction, so I took some evidence to him and he invited me to go with him to talk to them. You will be glad to know that Sheriff Taylor and I are best friends now. You no longer have to worry about his harassing me or tossing me out when I'm interviewing someone. I'm sure that's a relief off your mind."

Nick laughed out loud. "I didn't know I was that worried. If there is someone that can take care of herself, it's you. Are you going to tell me the information you gave him today?"

MIA TENROC

"That wasn't the deal last night. I said today, but not in the morning. Let's see what happens first. Anyways, what are your plans for today? I'm thinking I'll just hang out here in the room. I want to take a break and just read, relax, and talk to the family."

Nick was skeptical, "I'm glad you won't be getting into any trouble. We should have got up and went off early, but Kurt, Brian and I are going to the fishing hole with some beers and kicking back. It will give Kurt time to talk and think things over. If we went early in the morning, the fish biting might interrupt our conversation. I'm not sure how long we'll be. Just because he's out of jail doesn't mean he's in the clear. We have to keep working on the case. Let's go get some breakfast and say hi to Lola."

As soon as they walked in and sat down, Lola ran over, "Did you hear that Kurt was released? They say Kurt isn't cleared yet but still, it's a start. Was the information about GoGirl I gave you yesterday instrumental in that? I want to help Kurt. He's a good guy and suffers enough with that wife of his." She turned to Nick, "Sorry, I didn't mean anything by that." She then turned back to Jean, waiting for her answer.

"It sure did." Jean replied, "You have been very insightful and a great source of information. You can give yourself credit for being a great help." Lola took their orders and hurried off smiling.

SOCIAL DECEPTION MURDER

"GoGirl?" Nick waited an answer.

Jean just said, "You know the answer to the case but you don't want to see it. I do have some connection information that you don't have, but I'm going to wait until the end of the day. Let's eat so you can go out and torment the little fish."

Jean returned to her room and called Alan like she told Nick she would do. "Nothing new here, Mom," he said. "No one has contacted Timothy and Violet. Naomi and I see them every day. We went with them to a theme park yesterday because the store was closed. They spend a lot of time sitting on the balcony, watching the ocean in the daytime. They come over to the store in the evening. They are so happy. Naomi is taking them shopping today."

"Have you checked in with Josephine? She's been keeping me well-informed about the con man."

Alan replied, "We decided it was best for Jake and I to keep our distance from the sting. We are both easy to recognize and the two of us already tipped him off that we are onto his act. I wish I could be more involved. I do go to the team meetings and I plan to be there for the finale."

Josephine was Jean's next call. "Everyone is excited about the progress. We are letting Fannie do her undercover work and wear various costumes, but only when they receive the approval of Klaus. I think she has a crush on him. So far, she has been a blonde, redhead, brunette, and a raven."

Jean laughed, "Just like in real life. I have pictures of her when she tried all those hair colors. Blonde really does look the best on her. At least this is giving her something new and fun in her life. When is the next team meeting?"

"Tomorrow."

Jean then received an unexpected call. "Sheriff, how are you?"

"Jean, can you please come to the office about 3:00? I'm interviewing Glenda today. Her parents are coming in with her. I was wondering if you would like to join us. You seem pretty good at this interviewing business. I come across at being too old and too much of an authority figure for a young girl to open up to. I hope you don't mind my asking."

Jean was very pleased, "Not at all. I do happen to be older than you, but a teenage girl will more likely open up to a woman. I'm grateful to be there."

Outwood

Chapter 37 – The Night at the Campsite

Jean walked into Sheriff Taylor's office. He was sitting behind the desk and the scared teen sat between her parents. No one was smiling or happy. "This sure is a dreary scene. Can we move to the conference room across the hall?" Without waiting for an answer, Jean led the group to the room. The conference room had the standard long table that seated about 5 people on each side and two seats at the end. The walls were beige and only had two pictures of outdoor scenes decorating it. One end of the room had a screen on the wall, very typical and boring.

"I suppose so," answered the Sheriff a little late since they were already there. "What all do you have in your arms?"

MIA TENROC

The Sheriff sat at the head of the table with the parents on each side of him. Glenda sat next to her mom. Jean announced, "I checked in with my valuable source, Lola. She said the three of you are coffee drinkers and cherry pie eaters, so here is some for you." She unloaded a pie with plates and plastic silverware. "Glenda, why don't you move down here by me? We are the chocolate chip cookie eaters. I got your usual diet drink and I have my favorite, iced green tea." Jean motioned for Glenda to take the seat at the end of the table while she sat to her right. Jean's logic was that the end seats made people feel more powerful, and Glenda needed a boost of power. The other reason for the seating arrangement was to have the authority figures at the other end so it would make Glenda feel more like she is talking to Jean personally as a friend. Glenda's mother raised her head as if to object but then backed off.

When everyone was served, Glenda asked the Sheriff. "What do you want to ask me?" Glenda was so meek and worried, she was about to cry.

The Sheriff replied, "What can you tell me about Julie's murder?"

"Nothing," the soft voice answered, "She was alive when I left. I didn't find out about the murder until late the next day. I don't know a thing. Honest, I don't." Tears started to flow.

SOCIAL DECEPTION MURDER

The Sheriff looked at Jean, knowing he wasn't going to get anywhere with his usual method of interrogating people. Jean was glad he realized early on so maybe the interview could be saved. Jean turned to talk to Glenda directly, "Let's just ignore the people down there for now. It's just you and I enjoying our favorite treat and talking. Take all the cookies you want. We don't want to ask you questions yet because we don't know exactly what to ask. What I would like for you to do is just talk to me about what happened that night. You are not a suspect or anything. We are hoping you can reveal something that we haven't found out yet that might help us determine the truth. Do you know what verbatim means?" Glenda shook her no. Jean continued, "Verbatim means to repeat exactly. I know it is very hard to do, but can you just tell me what was said that night as much as possible? Let's begin with the arrival. Did you get there first? Who got there and when?"

Instead of answering, Glenda asked, "Aren't you Timothy's new stepmother? Is he doing ok? My older brother uses to play baseball with him."

Glenda's father was about to correct his daughter for not staying on subject, but Jean waved him off and shot an angry mother look his way. He fell silent. "Yes, I am his new stepmother. I sure hope Tim and his family like me and don't consider me one of those evil stepmothers like in the movies. His father and I are so happy he married such a wonderful girl like Violet. Do you know her?"

Glenda said, "Not really. I've gone to a couple of weddings at her family's barn but when she did come to school, I was a lot younger and we weren't in the same building."

Jean was glad to connect on a personal level and anticipated the next question. "Luckily, Timothy and Violet left for their honeymoon before the murder was discovered. The family discussed it and decided not to tell them about the death or how Kurt was considered a suspect. You only get one honeymoon, and we didn't want them to worry or have negative thoughts ruin their good time. Nick and I will be going down this weekend if we can get this cleared up and tell them then. That's one reason I would really appreciate your help. I know how much Tim loves Kurt."

With the personal connection made, Glenda began to ignore the others in the conference room. Her conversation was strictly to Jean. "I rode to what we call the campsite at 7:00 with Nancy and Joy. It was just starting to get dark. Tom and Andy were already there starting the campfire. Teenagers have hung out at that spot for years, even back in my parent's days." Jean shot a sideways glance hoping the parents wouldn't speak. Luckily, they didn't. "This is such a small town. In the winter, everyone is forced to either

SOCIAL DECEPTION MURDER

hang out at the diner or at someone's home. Since it is now close to summer, you can get out and enjoy being away from everyone at the campsite. Amber drove by herself and came in next. About 7:15, Julie and Adam arrived, late as usual. She likes to make an appearance. We all put lawn chair around the campfire and cooked s'mores. We didn't really talk about anything special. Just things like how we can't wait for school to be out. Adam talked a lot. He is planning to go away to college, and it seems like he is jealous of Scott because he was scouted and asked to go to a top school. Adam had to apply to colleges because his grades aren't very good. He had to accept at a small-time university. He did get on their football team and will be leaving soon for practice. He asked if Julie wanted to go with him."

Glenda stopped to sip her drink and then continued, "Julie was in a very bad mood. She told him no, that she wanted to go to Hollywood. I asked if she wanted to be an actress. She said maybe, but her real interest was in having lots of money and parties to go to. She said she found small towns too boring and wanted to live in a big city. Andy started to say what he was planning to do but Adam interrupted with some thought he had, which had nothing to do with the topic. It appeared Adam and Julie didn't care about what the rest of us wanted to talk about or our plans for the future. I feel like we were there to just watch their show. I got mad and asked Andy to continue. The rest of us talked about our future plans, with Adam and Julie not joining our conversation. Later, Adam attempted to kiss Julie, but she pushed him away. She shouted that he didn't need him to paw all over her. Andy asked if she was on her period or what. She told him to go home and that she would catch a ride back with Joy or Amber. Adam muttered some curse words under his breath and complained about what a waste of time it was for him to be with Julie as he drove off. Tom and Andy didn't know what to say or do, so Tom suggest that the two of them go watch a movie at his house. They asked if any of us wanted to come but we all declined. We could tell they really just wanted to get away and didn't actually want us to join them. Is any of this helping?"

Jean answered it did and how much she appreciated hearing it. Encouraged to continue, Glenda did so. "Julie started complaining about how Adam is so stupid that even though he had a good enough body, he would never go anywhere in life. Julie said she would never be happy with Adam. She claimed that she would be leaving on her 18th birthday in June and finally escape the prison life that her stepfather was trying to keep her in. Julie then asked to borrow Amber's phone. Amber wanted to know why. Julie admitted that she wanted to post some complaints about Scott. She figured Scott will become the big man on campus and that he might even earn money in the pros one day. She wanted revenge on him for dumping her. I found that confusing because Julie always told me that she dumped him. It was obvious that she became more upset when the truth slipped out. Amber refused Julie's request, pointing out that the last time she loaned her the phone, Julie posted horrible things about Kurt on #MeToo, and that while she removed it, Amber chastised Julie for spreading lies against men as a form of revenge. Julie shouted out that the men got what they deserved, that after all, they had no problem using women for their body so why not use what weapons that us women have against them? Amber told her that it was wrong but didn't argue any further right then. Julie started telling the rest of us about her life in Boston until recently. She bragged about using a fake ID and going out with rich and powerful men. Real men, not like the little boys in this town. She then told us her stepfather hated her and that she planned to destroy his life. I guess from what she said that he used to be some big-time banker and that they demoted him and force him to move here. Her parents made her change her name and tried to take away her freedom. There was one moment that was really weird: Amber asked her if her name used to be Meredith Morrow. We were all shocked, especially Julie. She laughed and at first asked why on earth Amber guessed that name before admitting that she was correct, that she did go by that name in Boston. Amber got up and left. The rest of us continued talking with one another for a little bit, but then Julie complained she was sick of all these time-wasting conversations and that we should leave too. We asked if she wanted a ride home and she said no, that she wanted to be alone. I figured she had a phone on her to call someone when she was ready to leave. We all left, and that was the last time I saw her."

Jean looked at Glenda's parents. They had been watching their daughter speak and when she concluded, they suddenly looked at each other and then hung their head. Glenda didn't notice their reaction. Their response told Jean that they recognized the name.

Jean pulled out a piece of paper. "Let's say this is the campfire. Here is the parking area by the road. Who was sitting where? Can you draw in where everyone parked their car?"

Glenda placed an X on the side of the campfire facing the road. "This was Julie and Adam's spot, with their back to the woods and facing the road. Amber was to the right. Joy, Nancy and I sat facing the woods. Tom and Andy were on the left between Adam and I." She drew the locations of the cars on the sheet.

Jean asked, "The car that was parked here, was it ever moved to the left side of the lot?"

Glenda corrected, "No. We got there first, so Amber's car was parked to the right. She never moved it until she left."

SOCIAL DECEPTION MURDER

Jean looked at the Sheriff. "Do you have any questions?"

Sheriff Taylor tried to speak but it sounded like a squeak. He took a drink of his coffee to clear his throat. "No, Glenda. You have been very helpful. Do you have anything else to add?"

Glenda shook her head. "Really? I felt like I was saying boring things."

Jean stood up and gave her a hug. "You truly have been helpful. I'm so glad I got to know you some while I was here." Both of her parents were dead silent. Jean wondered if they knew the gravity of the evidence given. "Do me a favor and take the rest of the pie and cookie home with you. Please don't tell anyone about this conversation. It's so depressing to talk about this murder case and it makes people uncomfortable, so I feel it is best to not discuss it. OK?"

Glenda returned Jean's hug and said, "Tell Timothy and Violet I wish them every bit of happiness."

Outwood

Chapter 38 – Fishing Trip (Wednesday)

Nick pulled up in front of Brian's house. He realized that he always parks on their side of the street instead of in front of his old house occupied by Kurt and Sylvia. Nick thought critically of himself for being petty. Both men came out of their homes as soon as he arrived. Brian brought the cooler to Nick's car. "Welcome," he said. "I'm really looking forward to today and getting away from everything."

Nick asked, "I brought water, beer, and ice. Is there anything else we need?"

Brian replied, "I have the finishing rods, bait, bug spray, and sunscreen. I brought you out a baseball cap since I didn't think you would be traveling with one."

SOCIAL DECEPTION MURDER

They watched as Kurt came over and put some folding chairs into Brian's truck. He also placed another cooler in the bed of the truck. Nick and Brian joined him, "Sylvia insisted on packing sandwiches for the trip. I also have some snacks."

Nick didn't say what he was thinking but it must have showed because Kurt said, "They are safe to eat. I'm sure of it. Sylvia is so grateful to you, Nick, for getting me out of jail. I don't think she would poison you right now. If you like, I will take a bite from each sandwich to make sure they are ok."

There was much laughter from all the men. Sylvia came out on the front porch and waved, "Have fun!"

In the truck, the three reminisced about the old days of fishing together. After setting up their gear, the talk turned to what fish might be biting this late in the morning. Then they sat in silence. There was an air of negativity from each man. It was Kurt who finally broke the ice, "I know why I'm angry. I was unjustly put in jail. I'm on suspended leave from my job, even though it is with pay. I'm going to look for another job because who can work for a boss that suspected you of committing a murder? At least I have some good news. Sylvia seems to be going along with the money guidelines. That being said, I really don't trust her to not sneak behind my back and go on a spending spree."

MIA TENROC

Nick tried to cheer his friend, "I don't believe Sheriff Taylor really wanted to put you in jail. He just couldn't see beyond the obvious clues that were planted. If he wouldn't have taken that action, people would accuse him of not doing his job or playing favoritism. You are a really good cop, it's all you ever wanted to be. Give it time. Maybe the hurt will dull and you can go back to your job."

Kurt asked, "Don't you think there will be townspeople that won't trust me?"

Brian replied, "This is a village of about 1,500 and everyone knows everyone. I believe more people were mad at the Sheriff for the arrest than not. I don't believe anyone will hold this against you, but let's just take it one day at a time. Nick, I've noticed an edge with you today. Is the honeymoon with Jean going well?"

There was real laughter again from all. "Jean has learned something about the case and refuses to tell me. I think my daughter knows more than she lets on because she keeps telling me to trust Jean. It's funny, the two of them got along alright but now suddenly, they are best buddies."

Brian agreed, "That is something to worry about, the two women ganging up on you."

Nick was sincere with his next statement, "I'm not shocked that we are involved in a murder investigation. Jean is like a magnet for murder cases. The reason I'm

SOCIAL DECEPTION MURDER

upset is that Sarah and Jean feel it's ok not to share information with me. Jean keeps secrets from me when she thinks I will stop her from doing something. Besides the fact that Jean and Sheriff Taylor are now buddies, Jean is also making a ton of phone calls to her sister, son, and everyone else in Abletown. She is up to something and I want to know what. Jean wouldn't lie to me, but it's like I have to guess the truth before she will admit it. What are you in a funk about, Brian?"

"I'm worrying over Amber. I know she hasn't been quite right since her brother died, but she is taking Julie's death a little too hard for me to understand. I think she only hung out with Julie because she feared what the nasty girl would do to her if she didn't. If anything, I thought she would've been relieved that she is gone. I talk to Anita a couple of times a day and she said that Amber won't quit crying. She is depressed to the point that Anita won't leave her alone. I don't know what to do. The Sheriff requested that I get Amber to come home. He is interviewing all the students that were at the campsite that night. Amber is the only one he hasn't talked to yet. Anita and Amber will come home tonight, and we will go to the interview tomorrow."

Kurt suggested, "I've never been one to believe in shrinks, but maybe it would do Amber some good to talk to a psychiatrist or someone. Maybe she has something she needs to get off her chest, but would be reluctant to tell you."

Nick responded, "Maybe you could talk with her. Well, maybe it'll be more along the lines of listening to her to make her feel calmer and more reassured. If you need Jean and I to come over, we would be glad to throw in our support." Nick suddenly felt like he had been hit in the head. Jean was right. Nick never explored the possibility that it might have been Amber because he loves her so much, but she was alone that evening, she had a key to Kurt's house, and she was the right size to match up with the footprints. He hoped it wasn't true, but Amber's overreaction might have been a clue. He would not say anything until he had more facts. If it is Amber, then Jean really was trying to protect him. He was wrong to doubt Jean.

Nick announced, "I feel really guilty saying those negative things about Jean. I know she truly loves me. I'm the one not being a very good husband. I think what we need is a second honeymoon. Maybe I can talk her into going to one of those remote cabins on a lake. That way, there will be no one there to get murdered."

Brian looked at Nick oddly. "I thought Jean hated fishing. Why do you think a remote cabin on a lake would be her idea of a second honeymoon?"

Nick couldn't wait to get back to Jean and discuss his new thoughts. Amber had the opportunity but what would've been the motive? He steered the conservation back to the old days.

Outwood

Chapter 39 – Jean's Wednesday

Josephine was ready to share an update. "Deanie got a call from Wilson. He asked if she could perform her magic again because he needed money for this month's expenses. He hopes that Deanie will turn $200.00 into $2,000.00. I went ahead and approved of the expense. I don't think he will take off with such a paltry amount. I think he'll keep on going until he gets at least $10,000.00 from Deanie. We had our meeting last night. Deanie feels that after the $2,000.00 mark, we should tempt him with a huge amount, but the rest of us are concerned about giving him too much before we are ready to spring our trap. After the meeting, we split up and took turns followed him until we found out where he is living. He is currently renting a room over on Park Ave. Belinda found an excuse to start a conversation with the owner. The only thing Belinda found out is that he answered an ad for the room. He gave 6 months of rent in cash upfront to the owner of the house, so they didn't run a credit check."

Jean cautioned. "That was a risk. I hope the owner doesn't tip him off that someone asked about him. I would not let Belinda go near that place again. I agree with the group about continuing to give smaller amounts of money before making the big jump. Does Klaus and Deanie have an idea on how to make the suggestion?"

"They do. Wilson said that he couldn't get to his money for a couple of weeks at the start. It's been less than a week, but they will use the excuse that Deanie, or should I say, Della needs to go out of town and that she wants to do one last bigger score for him before she leaves if he can provide the seed money."

Jean agreed, "That sounds good and plausible."

Josephine continued, "We each came up with a scripted play and acted them with Deanie while everyone else watched. Then we voted on which one to use. The next step was to guess how Wilson might respond. We spent the whole night going over all the possibilities. Klaus keeps saying that Deanie is a pro and can wing the part really easily, but I'm still worried about her safety. Can you think of anything else we might do?"

Jean assured her, "Josephine, you're doing a great job. There was never any indication about this con artist being violent. He just wants to take the money and run. If you start to see signs of possible danger, talk Nick's partner into going with you. Just try to do so without telling her about the reverse sting. There's a chance that she might not approve of our plan, and even if she does, she might leak it to Nick. It's nice to have a police officer in the family. Have there been any more responses from people he has cheated?"

"No. I'm sure there were probably more victims but either they haven't seen our efforts or just want to put it all in the past. Alan and Jake attended all the meetings, but we are making sure not to say anything in front of anyone outside the venture."

After the conversation with Josephine, the phone rang. It was Timothy. Jean held her breath as she answered. What if someone let the secret of the murder out to them? "Timothy, it's good to hear from you. Is the honeymoon going well? Is there anything you need?"

Timothy sounded apologetic, "Violet calls her mother and father every night and updates them on the daily activities. She thinks it's weird that you and Dad haven't been calling us. She thought I should call Dad, but he isn't answering his phone. Is there something wrong?"

SOCIAL DECEPTION MURDER

Jean felt a little relieved, "Tim, we just don't want to interfere with your time. We have total faith that if you need us, you will call. It certainly isn't a lack of love, just respect. If you want us to call, we will."

Tim assured her, "No. Why didn't Dad answer his phone today? I called him a couple of times."

"He's fishing, of course. Thankfully, he has Kurt and Brian to do that with. I'm sure they are just out of cell phone range. I don't know where their secret fishing spot is so I'm just guessing. Three rugged outdoor men like them know how to handle nature so I wouldn't worry unless he isn't back by dinner time."

Tim sounded confused, "I thought you were with the grandkids in the city."

Jean didn't want to tell a lie and was trying to think fast. "We've already spent time doing what the grandkids wanted us to do. Now it's time for Nick to enjoy some time with his friends."

Jean was glad that she didn't have to lie, and that Tim still didn't know the truth. She hoped that the rest of the day would go smoothly. Realizing it was already 1:30, Jean walked to the diner for lunch. As Jean entered, she noticed the owner/chef was at the counter taking off the clip. There were only two people in the place so the service should be quick. The chef nodded to Lola and then in Jean's direction. "Lola, it's time for your break."

Lola turned after following her boss's gaze, "Hi, Jean. So glad you came in. I'm on break now. Why don't I place the order for you and join you for lunch?"

Jean requested a bowl of chili and a side salad. Lola quickly put the food together and went to where Jean was seated, far from the couple by the door. Jean began the conversation, "Thank you so much for the recommendations of the pie and cookies for yesterday's meeting."

"Nick isn't having lunch with you?"

Jean replied, "Nick, Brian and Kurt are fishing right now. I'm not sure what that means for dinner. Do you think there will be a big catch and us having a fish fry tonight? I wasn't sure how much food to get."

Lola raised an eyebrow, "Most fishermen are already back by now. What time did they get started?" Jean told her about 9:00, which made Lola laugh. "Don't count on many fish tonight. You have to get up early to catch much. My bet is that they are using the fishing as a cover for sitting around and having a few beers alone. Those men are country boys. They know better."

Jean smiled, "Just so I don't have to go with them. I'm not a fishing person. The only part I like is sitting on the bank of the water. I hate baiting the hook. Casting is ok, but I'm always secretly wishing for everything to ignore me. I don't like reeling in the poor fish and even less taking it off the hook."

Lola then talked in a whisper, "There is a ton of gossip going around town and I was hoping you would confirm what is true and what is not."

Jean responded just as quietly, "I'm not in the loop so I don't know what is being said."

Lola felt Jean owed her since she had provided so much information on the investigation so far. "I hear that the girl we know as Julie Reddick is really Meredith Morrow, that disgusting tramp that led to the death of Amber's brother, and that Amber killed her for it."

Jean thought. "I can confirm for sure that Julie Reddick and Meredith Morrow are one and the same. As far as Amber is concern, she's been out of town and is coming back tonight. The Sheriff has interviewed the other young men and women that were at the campsite that night and will be interviewing Amber tomorrow morning."

Lola, still looking around as if she was being spied on, said, "There's talk of trouble in Outwood. The viewing for Julie is tonight. This town is one big family and after what she did to Brian, Anita and Amber, causing Victor's death and all, well, everyone is trying to decide what to do about the viewing. Most of them are saying they won't go, but some of them are thinking of throwing a party right at the place in front of the family to celebrate. You really don't know if Amber's the killer or not?"

Jean was truthful, "Even if I knew, which I'm not saying I do, that would be overstepping the line. I don't mind confirming the other. I'm sure we will all know in a few days."

After the meal, Jean walked into Sheriff Taylor's office to report the gossip she had just heard. She explained, "I live in a place roughly this size. The grapevine is not only quick, but usually quite accurate. I could tell from their reaction that Glenda's parents knew exactly who Meredith Morrow was. It appears someone has already told everyone around town that Julie Reddick is Meredith Morrow. I heard from Lola that most of the people are just boycotting the viewing tonight, but that others want to do more."

The Sheriff said with a regret, "Looks like I have no choice but to be there tonight just to make sure nothing happens."

Abletown

Chapter 40 – The Date at the Lake

Deanie was still at the park waiting for Wilson. She knew the others could hear if she spoke into the microphone, even if they couldn't answer. "Klaus, I can sense you are telling me to put on a smile. I'm going to try. I'm really finding this acting job to be a challenge, and I know that if it was on the silver screen, I'd be winning an award for it. I'd rather be cursing out the crook than looking happy and intrigued. Hey, speak of the devil." She saw Wilson arrive and adapted to her Della persona. "Hi, sweetie. I'm so glad to see you. How is your daughter doing?"

Wilson sat down and gave Deanie a kiss on the cheek. "You always brighten my day. I feel so blessed to have found you at this point in my life. I do apologize asking for your help again." He handed her the two hundred dollars. "I'm sorry that I keep taking advantage of our friendship like this so soon. I just need more to cover this month's bills. In another few days, I can get the money out of my investments and will have enough to pay my own way again. When the cash starts rolling in, I promise you to a night of dinner and dancing. Having you by my side means the world to me. This worry over my daughter's health would be too much to bear if it wasn't for you. I spoke to her just before coming here tonight and got good reports that the surgery went well. She is even up and moving some. Of course, now a days, they make people move right away."

Deanie at first gave the proper look of concern and then changed it to joy. "I'm glad you feel so supported by me, even though I really haven't done that much. I don't mind helping you one more time. It doesn't cost me anything to do the money changes. There is no danger of you not getting your money back and more."

The couple stood up and walked to the lake. There was a boat rental place where the watercrafts looked like swans. Wilson had a surprise for Deanie. The went off in a boat around the lake. Wilson brought a bag with him. He pulled out a sound system and played romantic music. He also had wine, crackers and cheese for them to snack on.

SOCIAL DECEPTION MURDER

Josephine was on the shore looking through binoculars, "I really don't like that they rowed out so far from reach. At the restaurants, we could easily rush in if she needs help."

Klaus tried to be optimistic despite his own discomfort, "Look on the bright side. Wilson hasn't caught on to her at all. My lovely little wife is playing him perfectly. The look on her face doesn't even come close to reflecting how she feels about the crook. I don't think anyone else in the world could pull off this acting job as well as she can."

They walked back to the van where Belinda, Fannie, and Steve were waiting. "There's no conversation, just music. I'm sure the mic is working correctly, or we wouldn't even hear that."

An hour later, the swan-shaped boat appeared at the dock. When Wilson extended his hand to help Deanie out, he pulled her close and kissed her passionately. He thought to himself that this lovely lady might be worth settling down with, someone to keep him in the style he liked living. Wilson spoke, "You are such a wonderful and gracious person. Please let me take you home tonight. I would very much like to be with you."

Deanie fell back onto the story, "I want us to date a few more weeks before I introduce you to my family. I have no doubt that my grandchildren would love you, and if stopped working out between us after you already met them, they would be disappointed."

The two of them walked back to the bench. Wilson turned the music on, bowed to Deanie and extended his arm. They began to dance. It went on for a long time and Josephine could sense the irritation arising in Klaus. "Relax, she's a professional. I bet that she's imagining you in her arms right now to pull this ruse off."

Klaus grumbled, "I've watched her kiss men on the stage many times. I don't get jealous, but to watch this horrible creep handle my precious gem like that makes my blood boil."

Outwood

Chapter 41 – The Hostile Viewing

Nick came to the room and immediately wrapped his arms around Jean. The moment Jean looked at his face, she knew that he figured out the answer to the murder. He apologized, "I'm so very sorry I was short with you today. Now I understand why you went to the Sheriff instead of me when you found something out. I know now it was probably Amber, but I don't know why."

Jean lovingly hugged her husband despite the outdoor fishing smells. "Julie Reddick used to go by the name Meredith Morrow. Her parents forced her to change it in order to hide her from her past." Nick stared at Jean in shock. "The court case that her mother brought against Victor had already been sealed, but I found some other documents and articles that hinted at a change in identity. I confirmed it by having Sarah check the school transfer records. I withheld what I discovered from you because I knew this would tear you apart inside. When you went over who had access to the gun, Amber never entered your mind. You focused on the other students Julie interacted with, but you never considered Amber in your reviews. I thought it was unusual that she first isolated herself and then left town, and that she was the only student to do so. I didn't decide it was her immediately, but when I questioned two of the girls that were at the campsite that night, I found out that Amber discovered that Julie and Meredith were the same person. Amber had a key to Kurt's house, and she knew that everyone else was still at the bachelor parties that night, so she was able to go in without being noticed. I'm so sorry. I know how much you love her."

Needing alone time, Nick said, "I need to shower and get this smell off me. Why don't you order in food?"

Sheriff Taylor was sitting outside the funeral home. The two tellers that worked at the back came up, "Our husbands didn't want us to come, but despite how horrible his wife and daughter are, Mr. Reddick is a good man." They stepped inside and went up to him but didn't go near the casket nor Mrs. Reddick. "We wanted to let you know that we are sorry for your loss

SOCIAL DECEPTION MURDER

and sorrow. You're a good person and I'm sorry that you are going through this."

Mrs. Reddick walked over, "Do you want to come over to see the body?"

The two women backed away to the door. "We're not staying. I doubt anyone else will be coming since everyone in Outwood knows now that she was Meredith Morrow. I'm sorry but the horrible scars she inflicted on the Johnson family and on this town are too great. We need to leave."

About fifteen minutes passed when Matthew and his parents entered. The Sheriff expected trouble and moved closer to the door so he could hear what was said. Matthew walked up to the body, touched it and laughed. "You got what you deserved, you heartless bitch." He then spat on her corpse.

A scream came out of Mrs. Reddick's mouth. Matthew's mother got in her face, "If you were a good parent, you would have gotten help or even locked up that psychopath you called a daughter. She led a life that benefitted no one and destroyed many. How dare you bring her to this town!"

Sheriff Taylor spoke up, "I understand your feelings but you need to leave." After the three departed, the Sheriff told the Reddicks about the malicious prank Julie pulled on Matthew. Mr. Reddick understood their rage, but Mrs. Reddick only became more hysterical.

"I can't have my daughter buried here," she told the funeral director. "I want the body cremated and I want to take my daughter's ashes with me when I leave. It's hard to say what this demented place would do to her grave."

Outwood

Chapter 42 – Amber's Return

Jean and Nick had eaten and were curled up on the bed relaxing when the phone rang. "Nick, It's Brian." Brian was crying. Nick had never seen Brian shed a tear before, so it shocked him. "Nick, I need help. Can you come? Wait, before you do, would helping me create a problem with your job?"

Nick stated, "Brian, we know it was Amber." Brian didn't even breathe. "Jean and I are on our way. We will always be there for you and Amber."

Jean was out of the car before Nick could turn it off. She could smell the smoke from the firepit in the backyard. Amber stepped around the corner of the house when Jean wrapped her arms around her. "You poor darling. You have been through so much." She continued to hold Amber close when Nick came up and encircled both of them in his arms. "We love you, Amber, and we are here for you."

"Even after what I did?" The three walked to the backyard. Amber sat between Jean and Nick on the swing.

Jean said, "Amber, the location was surrounded by hemlock. Why didn't you get her to eat some instead of shooting her? That's what I would have done."

Nick gave a dirty look to Jean, "You're not helping." Amber giggled.

"I'm trying to let Amber know that I felt that she was totally justified. The law protects criminals like Julie more that it does their victims. That's what I would have done anyway, the hemlock I mean."

Nick stared, "You would kill someone?"

Jean had to think on that one, "No, probably not. I would have filed a civil suit against her and made mental treatment for Julie and her mother as one of the costs, instead of just money. What a terrible mother to allow her daughter to be so evil. It's almost as if she deliberately encouraged her to be that way."

Amber was grateful that Jean understood her emotions. "I didn't know what I was doing. She was so wicked. When she started talking about ruining Scott's life, I began remembering all of the things that happened to Victor. But then she mentioned her life in Boston and I instantly had this gut feeling that she was Meredith, the girl that killed my brother. I asked, and she laughed and confirmed it. I drove home angrily. I wanted to stop her from ruining any more lives, but I didn't plan to kill her. I just took the gun to scare her. When I returned to the campsite, I told her I was Victor's sister and that I blamed her for his death. Even with the gun pointed at her, she laughed and told me what absolute losers he and I were. I couldn't take anymore: her laughing, her mockery, her malice. So, without thinking, I just pulled the trigger."

Kurt's voice was heard, "Why did you use my gun? Did you want them to blame me?"

The three of them turned to see Kurt and Sylvia standing by the house. "No, Uncle Kurt." said Amber softly. "I would've never let them do anything to you. I would have confessed first. I'm sorry they arrested you. I didn't plan to kill her, honest. But after I shot her in rage, I didn't know what to do. I couldn't think straight. Later, I thought that maybe they might end up blaming Sylvia and that I would be freeing you from her too. I would have told you the full truth if they did, Uncle Kurt, and then let you decide what to do." The fact that Amber would say 'Uncle Kurt' but never 'Aunt Sylvia' wasn't missed by Jean or Nick.

Sylvia began to cry, "You think I'm so evil that I deserve to go to jail? You think Kurt hates me so much that he would want to be rid of me?"

Amber became upset again, "I didn't do it to frame you, but I doubt anyone would've cared if that ended up happening. You have always been horrible to both Uncle Nick and Uncle Kurt. Everyone knows you ruined Uncle Nick's life by getting pregnant on purpose. The only reason you're with Uncle Kurt in the first place is because he came into money, and you had already dried up Uncle Nick's by that point. You aren't a partner in any relationship. You're a manipulate, controlling, materialistic, greedy leech. You never loved anyone but yourself! You're just as wicked as Julie was!"

Sylvia turned and ran into her house bawling. Kurt stayed a minute. "Amber, I'm with you in any way I can be. I understand why you did it, but it wasn't right. I guess I better go home now unless you need me."

Brian asked Nick, "What happens now? What will they do to Amber?"

Nick said, "She is just 16, so she's still considered a minor. It's wasn't first degree and it's not like she murdered with an evil heart. She might be able to plea temporary insanity. I know a good lawyer in Minneapolis from when I was on the police force there.

SOCIAL DECEPTION MURDER

I will see if he is still practicing and ask if he could come here to represent Amber if you like."

Anita, who was very quiet through all this, asked, "Do you think it will ever be ok?"

Nick walks up to Anita and gave her a hug. "Yes, I truly believe that it eventually will."

Outwood

Chapter 43 – Mr. Reddick's Visit (Thursday)

Amber was still tense from the conversation earlier. Anita suggested that sleep would be the best thing. Amber asked Anita, "I don't want to be alone. Can you please sleep in my room?"

When they were in the house, Jean said, "I think I will call some friends on the phone. If you will excuse me, I'll be in the front room if you need me."

Brian and Nick both knew Jean was giving the two men a chance to talk alone and were grateful for that. A couple of hours later, Nick came in and put a cover over Jean who was asleep on the couch. She woke, "Did you want to go to our room?"

SOCIAL DECEPTION MURDER

Nick got a separate cover and laid back in the recliner, "If you don't mind, I think we need to stay here for tonight. I want to be there for my friends every step of the way. They need me right now. Also, Brian asked if I could stay until things were settled."

Jean sat up some, "How long will that be? You think the trial will come that soon?"

Nick smiled, "Well, maybe not the whole time but at least through the arrest period and arraignment. I might be coming back up here if there is court action. The attorney we hire will have to decide if they want a court action or negotiation instead."

Nick was able to fall asleep. It was quiet, except for Brian's pacing at times, until about 8:00 when the doorbell rang. Nick jumped up to answer, waving Brian back when he was coming down the stairs. Jean looked out the window, "It's Mr. Reddick, Julie's stepfather."

Nick paused, "Should we answer?"

Jean assured him, "He's ok. If it was his wife, I wouldn't open it."

Nick opened the door but didn't sound too welcoming, "Can I help you?"

Mr. Reddick asked, "Could I speak to Brian, please? Say, are you Jean's husband?"

Nick looked curious. "You know my wife?"

MIA TENROC

Before Mr. Reddick can answer, Brian was already stepping to the door. "Can I help you?"

Mr. Reddick already knew Brian since he was a customer at the bank, "Brian, I can't tell you how sorry I am for all that you are going through. I'm taking my wife to the airport today. I was only Julie's, or if you prefer, Meredith's stepfather for about three years. I stayed out of her life and let her mother handle it. I had no idea what was going on. Even though she wasn't my child, I feel I should take responsibility. I've made a decision. I have set up an account at the bank which one of the tellers, Polly Alexander, will handle. It is the Amber Support Fund. I've heard rumors in town that most people believe she might need someone to represent her. I've put in $100,000.00 to start with in the account. If you feel Amber will need a good attorney to be with her during the interview with the police, you can turn the bill in at the bank and it will be paid. Even if Amber didn't do it, I hear she's taking it really hard. The money can be used in other ways, such as professional counseling. I can't take back what has happened. I'm not doing this to ease my mind. I'm doing this because my family have cost you so much that it can't be repaid. I won't see you going broke getting Amber whatever help she needs. I'm trying to do what is right. If more money is needed, Polly will contact me. I'm taking a couple of weeks off and working with my bank about a transfer. The last thing

SOCIAL DECEPTION MURDER

the people in Outwood needs is to see me every day. If you need me, just call Polly."

Brian just extended his hand and said, "Thank you."

Mr. Reddick turned to leave when Jean came to the door, "I'm sorry for what happened last night. I do understand why it happened, but some things are better left unsaid. Are you ok?'"

Mr. Reddick gave Jean a half smile, "I'm glad I have a pre-nuptial agreement. Three years of my life wasted. I've made some very stupid mistakes. Hopefully, I will be a little wiser in the future." He got into his car and left.

Nick looked at his wife but before he could say anything, Brian suggested they called the attorney's office to see if they would take the case. Amber, who had been sitting on the top step listening to the conversation at the door, turned to go back upstairs to the bathroom. Jean heard the shower turn on. What a horrible day that was ahead for the child.

Anita headed to the kitchen to start breakfast; Jean joined her. Nick and Brian came in after they got off the phone. Brian related the conversation to Anita, "Mr. Inlet accepted our case. He told me that he wouldn't be able to get up here today but that we could do a conference call with him in an hour with Amber included and he will instruct us on what to do. We can even do the conference call when Sheriff Taylor interviews Amber at noon. I contacted the Sheriff right after and he agreed to it."

Nick asked Jean about her statement to Mr. Reddick, "I talked to Lola last night." Everyone rolled their eyes.

Jean said, "At least her gossip is usually right." They told the others about Matthew and his family's visit to the viewing

Nick and Jean followed Brian's car to the police station. At first, Nick felt that neither Brian nor Anita should be driving but they insisted they were fine and that they might want to stay at the police station overnight. All along the route were signs saying, "We Love You Amber", "We are by your side". Some even said, "Thank You". The town was showing their support, which greatly lifted Amber's spirit.

At the station, Nick and Jean joined the family in the conference room with no complaint from the Sheriff. The conference call occurred with Amber admitting to the crime but planning to plea temporary insanity. The Sheriff concurred with the final decision. "I've used what little influence I have with the court system to escalate the hearing for bond. I talked to the DA and we all agreed that since you came and turned yourself in, the recommendation will be no bail needed and that you be released to your parent's custody. We don't feel that you are a danger to anyone else, and we trust your word that you won't leave the county. The only restriction is that you must be in the presence of one of your parents at all times. You can arrange with the school to have your final tests at home. We think it is best that you don't go to school, church, or any place with a large gathering of people."

Outwood

Chapter 44 – Breaking the News

Feeling more assured by their company, Brian said, "Nick, Jean, I can't thank you enough for being by our side. I know it was a long night. I understand if you want to go off and get some sleep in a bed or relax."

Nick left only after Brian promised to call if they needed anything. "I think it's time to be honest with Timothy." Back at the hotel, Nick called the other members of the family to tell them what happened. He learned that Sylvia called each of their children and sobbed about what Amber had said.

Sarah responded, "Amber was so wrong to say and feel those things about Mother." Nick wouldn't comment because he wanted to keep peace with the

SOCIAL DECEPTION MURDER

family, but he actually felt grateful that Amber expressed how wrong Sylvia and the kids had treated him. James and John made no comments about their feelings on the issue. They just confirmed that Sylvia told them the story. It was agreed that it was now time to tell Tim what happened since there was no longer any more risk of danger or additional surprises for the family.

Jean called Alan to find out today's schedule for the newlyweds. They just came in from the beach and were cleaning up to go to Alan and Naomi's store for gaming. Alan was not shy about expressing his thoughts, "If that was you under arrest, I would've been livid if I was kept in the dark the whole time. I'll head over to their condo and be there when you tell them the story. Naomi doesn't mind watching the store. It usually doesn't get busy here until 6:00."

Alan texted when he arrived and was with Tim and Violet so Nick could call. Nick started, "Tim, Violet, I hope you won't be upset when I tell you the news. Everything is fine now, but I would rather you here what happened from me instead of through town gossip." Nick told them about Amber killing Julie with Kurt's gun and the aftermath that followed. He omitted the part about Amber's chewing out Sylvia. He thought even she wouldn't be that low to cry on Tim's shoulder. "I knew Kurt didn't do it. He was never in danger. Your brothers, sister and I decided not to tell you since we knew it would all work out. Besides, we felt that you two should be enjoying your honeymoon, not worrying over something you had no control over. Alan told me that he didn't agree with our decision. If you feel that way too, I apologize, but I had to do what I thought was right."

Tim became very upset, "I'm not mad because you didn't tell us. I'm worried about Amber. She has always been a close friend. I don't want something bad to happen to her."

Nick tried to assure him, "She described the events that happened, and she really was driven to the point of insanity, even if only temporarily. Everyone is on her side. Being a minor, they probably will not push for anything too severe, and they will seal the records so it won't follow her the rest of her life."

Violet asked, "Jean, do you have anything to add to the story?"

Nick didn't let her answer, "Jean was telling Amber that she should have used hemlock to kill her, so I don't think we need Jean's opinion."

Alan laughed, "That's definitely sounds like my mother!"

Nick concluded, "I hope none of this ruined your honeymoon. Everything will be ok. I'm staying close

SOCIAL DECEPTION MURDER

with Brian, Anita, and Amber to help them in any way possible. This is my field of expertise."

Alan was texting with Jean, "Didn't I say you needed to marry a detective? Didn't I say murder would follow you?"

Jean ignored his comments and texted back. "Stay with them until you are sure they are ok."

After the call, Alan turned to Tim and Violet, "Do you want or need to talk about any of this?"

Tim assured him, "We are ok. We are very sad for everyone, especially Amber, but things will be ok. I'm kind of glad Dad didn't let us know. I would have gone on home to be by Kurt's side even if I couldn't do anything. As long as he knows that, I'm good."

Nick then had a conference call with James, John, and Sarah. "I've got my phone on speaker so Jean can join in, but I don't want any of you having your phones on speaker because I don't want the grandkids to overhear. Amber confessed to the murder of Julie Reddick. Sarah helped Jean discover that Julie Reddick's original name was Meredith Morrow, the person responsible for Victor's death." There was a collected breath as the shock settled in the three of them.

MIA TENROC

Sarah was the first to speak, "Even after I knew that fact, I still couldn't believe our sweet Amber doing such a thing."

Jean explained, "Amber says she took the gun to scare Julie but that she didn't plan to kill her. Julie was on an attack campaign against Scott Surly to destroy his life. After all, he'll be a big man on campus next year. His football skills are sure to escalate him to the pros. Julie thought that he was going to take her along for the ride. However, Scott realized how destructive and mentally ill Julie was and broke it off with her. He had hoped that letting her say that she broke up with him would pacify her, but it wasn't enough. Amber couldn't stand to see another person's life ruined, so she threatened Julie. Julie dismissed the threat as a big joke, and then said what a loser Victor was and laughed in Amber's face. It was temporary insanity. Mr. Reddick is paying all legal expenses and promised to help Amber rebuild her life. He doesn't want her prosecuted, but he can't stop that from happening."

James joined in, "That is quite a good man. Most people wouldn't have realized what Amber went through. I have total respect for him."

John asked, "Dad, I know you and Jean did so much for Kurt. Is there any way we could repay you?"

Nick had the answer already in mind. "Yes. Our hope was to spend time with our grandchildren. At their request, we missed out on that. I don't want to leave town in case Brian or Anita needs us for the next couple of days. I want time not only with the kids but with the three of you as well. John or Sarah, could you put on a last-minute picnic and have everyone attend tomorrow? One other condition, I don't want Kurt or Sylvia there. Not to be rude, but the grandkids act even more unnatural with those two around. The reason we wanted to take them away was so they could be themselves around us."

James immediately agreed, "You got it, Dad. We will have food on the grill, cornhole, a little softball, everything you like."

"What about badminton and water balloon fights? I helped solve this, so I want my favorite things too," Jean inserted.

That created a laugh. John responded, "Sure thing. Not to be rude, Jean, but it's so odd to have a parent that doesn't mind getting all wet to have fun."

James suggested, "If one of you, John or Sarah, will put up with my family for the night, we can go to that one lake on Sunday where we can rent canoes and paddleboards."

Nick started to ask what food take, but Sarah stopped him, "No. It will be easy for me to put together some potato salad, sandwiches, chips and other things. If John is taking care of Saturday, I will do Sunday."

Nick insisted on buying the drinks and ice. This was a plan that made everyone happy.

Abletown

Chapter 45 – An Unexpected Proposition (Friday)

Armed with the $2,000.00 to give to Wilson, Deanie was getting dressed for her next date. "Klaus, I think Wilson might actually be falling for me."

Klaus laughed as he got off the bed and walked over to stand behind his wife at the mirror. "A man would have to be a fool not to love you. I admit I can't stand you being around him. I know you are acting, but he isn't. I wouldn't be surprised if he didn't ask you to marry him."

"Not this soon, he wouldn't. I have to admit I wonder if my acting is good enough at times, but if you really think Wilson will propose to me, it must be spot on."

MIA TENROC

They left for the meeting. Josephine and Mike were setting up at a pavilion not far away. Belinda, Fannie and Klaus would be in the parking lot in the van. Klaus said, "Fannie is bringing the food and drinks for us. We are parked in such a way that we can get in and out of the van to use the restrooms if needed without being seen by you. Fannie is one of those eccentric thinkers, so I wonder what our food will be. I also think she has a little crush on me. Did you notice that?"

"She has good taste, my dear, but she also knows we are happily married. She's just a natural born flirt." Deanie continued, "I wonder why Wilson wants to meet at the park by the mall today? It seems like an unusual place to go for courtship."

Wilson was already at the table when Deanie arrived. He stood and gave her a hug and quick kiss, more like a French greeting instead of romantic. It was more gentlemanly that way. "My dear, it is so good to see you."

While eating, Deanie started the conversation as usual with, "How is your daughter doing?" She received assurance that she was rehabbing fine. The usual inquiry about their fictional families continued the polite conversation throughout the meal. Deanie then slipped the envelope containing the money to Wilson. "Here is the $2,000.00. The time for money exchange is extremely good right now but that can change at any moment. My daughter wants me to go with them on a short vacation. School is out and the day camp program they will attend this summer doesn't start for two weeks. We wanted to use this time to do something different and exciting for the children. We plan to leave next Wednesday, so the two of us will only have Monday and Tuesday to be together. Hopefully this money will keep you through until your investments become available to you."

With the meal completed, Wilson steered Deanie into the mall. "The heat is merciless today; I thought walking in the mall would be nice." Soon they were in front of a jewelry store. "If you could pick any ring in the store, which would it be? Do you like rings that have a large single stone or a cluster of smaller ones, like this one here that forms a flower?"

Deanie replied, "I don't have any intentions of buying a ring. I haven't worn one since my husband died. I know some women like to keep wearing their rings in memory of their loved one, but I found that every time I looked at mine, I kept hoping he would come back. I took them off so I could move on with my life."

Wilson looked deep into her eyes, "Della," he said. Despite how long the ruse had been going, Deanie still had to remind herself that Della was her fake name in the dating app. Wilson didn't often call her by name, usually preferring to use "My Dear" or "Sweetie" instead. Wilson continued, "Della, I know this is rushing things, but I can't help myself. I never considered marrying again, but after meeting you, I have changed my mind. I look forward to nothing but being with you each day. I think it is time to meet the family and start making plans for a life together. I can't imagine ever leaving you. I'm not saying we will buy the ring today, but I want to know your taste so that when I do officially propose that I present you with the ring you approve of. I'm announcing my intent to be with you always."

Deanie was quite taken back. One of the things she learned from the other victims was that he never wanted to meet the family. None of them mentioned about shopping for a ring either. Deanie's hesitation wasn't missed by Wilson who asked, "You're not happy about me announcing my intentions?"

"I'm just so surprised. At first, you said that you didn't want to meet the family until you were sure. It's not been but a few days that we have known each other." Which was a true statement by Deanie.

Hugging her close, Wilson responded, "I've never been so sure in my life. I know it hasn't been long. I'm not trying to pressure you, but I want you to know that my true hope is to be with you." His statements were quite sincere. He actually liked Della a lot. She was

SOCIAL DECEPTION MURDER

pretty and interesting, and with her ability to bring in an endless supply of money, he would never need to pull off a con again. He only had to think of how to introduce the daughter who never existed.

Deanie continued the game, trying to show the right amount of enthusiasm. "You're right, Wilson. I like the flower cluster. It would represent all the people that loved me: my daughters, grandchildren, and you." Now the kiss became romantic. A representative from the store had been watching and encouraged them to come in to try on the ring. Deanie then tried to promote the idea of a big cash-in day to fund their new life, "Where would we live? I don't want to be far from the grandchildren so they could come over after school until their mother got home. I talked to a lady recently that lives a few blocks away. She said she was putting her house on the market. Would you object to my asking her to let us see the house when I get back or is it too soon to start making plans like that?"

Wilson wondered if he misunderstood her hesitancy before. He was unsure. "Let's meet tomorrow and maybe we could drive by and see it."

Afterwards, they walked around the mall for about an hour, comparing taste for various household items like bedding and furniture. Deanie couldn't wait to meet with those listening to find out if she made a mistake in inventing this script. Where on earth would the house be that she could show him?

Outwood

Chapter 46 – Interrupting the Fun (Saturday)

Nick was greeted with loud laughter and love as the grandchildren were pulling him into the house. "Grandpa! We are so glad to spend the day with you. Games are all set up in the backyard."

"I get to be Grandpa's partner." Proclaimed one.

Another argued, "No fair. Everyone knows Grandpa is the best at all the games. I want to be his partner too."

Nick settled the matter by proclaiming, "We will do the games in round robin format, so everyone gets to be my partner once, because I want to be partners with all of you."

Jean was hugged and kissed by all the grandchildren as well, but the biggest hugs came from James, John, and Sarah. There were many whispers of thank you from all three. The backyard was a paradise of fun with all the toys. There was a huge table loaded with food. Jean went for the watermelon first. Noon time was cooking on the grill, with all the men making suggestions on the best way to cook the meal. Games resumed with the water balloon toss. There, you only could choose one partner. Everyone facing the house threw to their partner, who then took one step back and returned the throw. Every break created laughter and teasing for the loser.

The teams returned to cornhole when Jean phone rang. She wasn't up for another round, so she went into the house to accept the call from Josephine. "I want to compare ideas on how to proceed." Josephine related the details of the marriage proposal from Wilson to Deanie. "We heard the stories from the other victims, and no one said anything about Wilson asking them to marry him. We tried to cover every scenario that might come up, but we never even considered him asking her hand in marriage. Deanie had to improvise. The house idea she came up with seems good because it would make him want to get more money soon, but we don't know where to get the house."

Jean made a call before getting back to Josephine "Jo, do you remember Malia Adams? She is a realtor

SOCIAL DECEPTION MURDER

I've known for years. I called her if she could find the type of house that was similar to what Deanie described. I was completely honest with her about the plan. She offered to meet Wilson and Deanie at a house she had listed tomorrow around 2:00. I told her I didn't want her to get involved any further than she has to, so she will just open the house for them and step away until all was clear. One of you will pretend to be the neighbor who knows Deanie. Who do you think should play that part?"

"Belinda would be good. She hasn't been the inside spy on many of the meetings so I don't think he will recognize her."

Nick came up behind Jean, "What are you doing in here? It's your turn to play."

Jean quickly ended the call saying, "I got to go. Talk to you later."

Nick looked suspiciously at Jean. "I know you are up to something. Are you going to tell me?"

Jean replied no as she headed out the door, ignoring the hands on the hip with a hard stare that Nick gave her.

Abletown

Chapter 47 – Breaking Down (Sunday)

The team worked hard in the morning predicting possible scenarios that might come up and how to respond to them. Despite their efforts, Deanie was still very nervous about this upcoming date. Klaus noticed her hesitation and suggested, "If you are not up for this, just say so." Deanie claimed she was ready to go.

At the house, Wilson noticed the For Sale sign. After being introduced to Belinda, who used the name of Beatrice for the con, he commented, "I thought you were going to let Della know before you placed the house on the market."

Beatrice explained, "I didn't think she was serious, and besides, it was a couple weeks ago that we talked about it. Let me show you around the house. There's

SOCIAL DECEPTION MURDER

not too much to see, just two bedrooms and one bath. Here is a nice screened-in porch. Some people want a more modern kitchen and a great room, but this is more your typical home for this area. What do you think, Della?"

Belinda noticed that Deanie was off her game and gave her a nudge. Deanie attempted to get into character. "I personally like the kitchen being separate from the rest of the house. I don't want to see the mess I need to clean up when relaxing in my recliner. I dislike stainless steel appliances as they show every fingerprint. I like how it isn't too big, less to keep clean."

Wilson expressed his opinion, "I totally agree with you, my dear. I can really enjoy having my morning coffee and reading on the screened porch. I also like the two-car garage. I don't like it when a car is sitting out getting sap from the trees on it. What is the house priced at?"

Belinda as Beatrice said, "I only have $175,000.00 on it. I have to admit I received an offer already, but it was way too low. I turned it down without a counteroffer. The realtor said she thought it was just a test and that they would make a serious offer soon. It has only been on the market for a few days, so I plan to wait for now. From what I hear, houses are only on the market a few days in this area. I'm sure I will get the full price soon."

Wilson asked to speak to Della alone. "Do you really want this house? I like it but I can't tell for sure about you." Deanie as Della admitted she did like it. Wilson turned to who he knows as Beatrice, "This is a sudden decision for us. Only yesterday did we decide we might want to purchase a house. We haven't discussed finances, but I would be willing to pay full price. Can you give me a couple of days to come up with the money? Please call me if you get an offer before I get back to you."

As Wilson was writing down his number, Deanie came unglued, "If you want to buy this house for yourself, Wilson, that's fine, but I can't promise marriage or that I will live here."

She started to cry and ran from the house. Wilson and Belinda both were in shock. Belinda tried to create a cover for the unexpected outburst. "I didn't even know Della was dating someone. She had been refusing to date since her husband died. I think this might be too soon for her. You know how planning to marry or live with someone is a huge emotional commitment."

Wilson looked crushed. "I was afraid that I was pushing too fast. It's true that we've only been together for a couple of weeks. I just fell so head over heels in

SOCIAL DECEPTION MURDER

love with her. I guess I'm being rude with being so aggressive in my pursuit of her. I just thought she would appreciate my honesty."

Belinda thought that was ironic considering he was never sincere before. There was nothing honest about this whole relationship. "You need to think about this for a few days. Maybe if you go ahead and get the house, Della will come around. I'll tell you what, I have the house actually priced low. If you get financing in the next week and can close the deal soon, I will let you have the house for $168,000.00. That way, if things don't work out between you and Della, you'll have enough equity in the house to sell it immediately. You could end up getting a big payoff on your investment. I have to be in another state starting in two weeks for my new job."

Wilson like that thought. He believed that even if his plan with Della didn't work, he could still end up with a big payday from this whole situation.

Abletown

Chapter 48 – Finishing the Sting

Deanie ran to the van hidden a block down the street. With Belinda detaining Wilson, there was no chance of him following Deanie or seeing the van. Klaus asked, "What's going on? What happened? Are you ok?" Deanie just sat there crying and wouldn't speak.

Belinda called Josephine's cell phone and told her the conversation she just had. Josephine suggested they all go to the funeral home where they held their meetings. Deanie would only say, "I'm sorry! I just want to go home!"

Josephine got out and went to the backup car that was Belinda's and waited for her return. "Did Deanie say what happened or why she cried and ran away?"

SOCIAL DECEPTION MURDER

"No. She wouldn't say a word except that she wanted to go home. Klaus said he will call and let us know when Deanie has calmed down. We will have an emergency meeting then. I can't figure it out, but she has been acting strange ever since Wilson announced his intention to propose to her."

At their house, Klaus got Deanie settled on the veranda and poured two glasses of red wine from the box brand they liked to drink. He never said a word nor asked a question. He just showed kindness and patience. Deanie held up her empty glass and he refilled it. "It must really be rough for you to have a two-glass night," he joked.

After the first sip off the second glass, Deanie was ready to talk. "I know Wilson is a horrible person, the way he conned those poor women out of their money and played on their feelings. My sorrow for them is what made me want to do this acting job. I realize now that I'm stooping to his level. He should feel terrible for his past actions. I know how bad I feel about my actions. I would never hurt someone on purpose. I'm not an evil person but right now, I feel like one."

This was the first time that Klaus thought of the emotional repercussions of the plan. "I'm so sorry. I never thought about how this would affect you. You don't have to continue. I'm sure everyone will understand. I will talk with the others and maybe they can end this with just getting Wilson somewhere and letting the victims tell him how he destroyed them or their families. I'm sure he won't ever find you with us being somewhat retired, plus we were careful to use a different car that didn't include the right plates. We should be fine. Let me call and tell the others that we're opting out."

Deanie stood, "I can't do that to them. I was the one that insisted on doing this acting job. They asked for you to call them so we could have a meeting. Please go ahead and arrange it. I will go with you to explain my actions. We can decide from there. Besides, I've had a dozen calls from Wilson since then. I want them to the messages too."

At the funeral home, the meeting started with Deanie explaining her actions. She then played the calls for all to hear.

"Della, this is Wilson. I don't understand what's wrong. Please call me." "Della, I really care about you. Beatrice said I was pushing too much. I'm so sorry. I will give you time and space." Most of the calls were just a plea for a return call. The final one was, "Della, Beatrice made me a good deal on the house. I'm thinking of buying it. If you would only let me know that you will see me again. My investments have come in. If you are willing to do the exchange thing one more time, I could pay cash for it. Then we can just date, and I can give you all the time you need."

The phone rang before the discussion could start. Deanie didn't answer it but the voicemail said, "Della, let's meet tomorrow morning at 8:00 at Ocean Front Restaurant. I have reserved the private room so we can talk. We really need to talk. I will bring the money along in case you want to help me buy the house."

Josephine took the phone and texted back, "I will be there." She said to the group, "This is perfect. I will let the other victims know to get there before 8:00 and to hide until he has settled into the room. Deanie, you don't need to come. I will be the one waiting for him. I understand now how this is making you feel, but I don't want to let the others miss the opportunity to at least express to Wilson, or William or whoever he pretends to be, their contempt for him. I think I will pretend that I'm your daughter and that I checked him out after he so heavily pursued you and discovered he was a con man. That way he can't blame you. I will tell him that I warned you yesterday and that is why you left crying, that you had actually hoped that he would be for real."

Deanie said, "I think I should be there. I won't say anything. I'm torn; I don't want to continue but I feel an obligation to see it through."

Josephine assured her, "If you want to be there, then come. If you don't want to, we understand. At least we can see this through either way. Thank you for doing all you did to stop this evil man. You have done a good service."

Outwood

Chapter 49 – Picnic at the Lake

Jean's phone rang, waking Nick up from his nap. "Hello?"

Josephine asked, "Hi Nick. Just calling to speak to Jean for a minute. Is she around?"

Nick had joy in his voice and explained, "She's on a paddleboard right now in the middle of the lake. It has been such a great day." After encouragement from Josephine, he continued. "Three of my children and all the grandchildren are spending the day at the lake with Jean and me. One son brought his boat. We have been waterskiing, canoeing, and paddleboarding. We brought a spread of food. After a few hours of fun and a good meal, I fell asleep on the quilt we had spread out to sit on. I was just going to sit here while the little ones took a nap but now, I'm the only one here. I can see everyone, so all of us are safe. I can have Jean call you when she gets in or if you have a message, I will deliver it."

"No, just have Jean call me," Josephine requested.

Nick wanted to take a chance of finding out what was going on in Abletown. "This has been a great day. Fantastic weather with blue skies and nice temperature. I will be so sorry when we head back on Tuesday. The case here is about over. We are going with Brian, Anita, and Amber tomorrow when they meet with their attorney and the district attorney. How is the case you're working on coming along?"

The last time Josephine heard, Jean hadn't told Nick anything. Does he know or is he fishing? She decided to not take the chance. "Not really working on a case here. Just doing what the water aerobics team normally does."

Knowing she wasn't going to spill the beans, Nick ended with, "Jean probably doesn't realize how many core muscles she is using. I bet she will be sore tomorrow. I will have her call when she gets to shore."

About a half hour later, Jean flopped down on the quilt next to Nick. "I didn't realize how far out I went. I was hoping you would bring the boat to rescue me."

Nick laughed, "I had no way of knowing you needed to be rescued." He gave her a kiss. "Your sister called. I told her you would call back later. I tried to get her to tell me what you are up to behind my back. No luck though, she didn't fall for my lead in. Are you going to tell me?"

Jean led with a kiss. "I sure love you." Nick was still staring so Jean continued, "We aren't in a murder investigation or anything like that. We are sure we are within the law but just in case we aren't, I'd rather not involve you." Nick continued the look. Jean finally relented a little, "Things will end tomorrow for the case here and the action there. I will tell you either tomorrow night or Tuesday, if you really must know." That was enough to satisfy Nick.

James came over to ask, "What is your schedule for the rest of the time here?"

Nick sat up, "We are going to the hearing tomorrow morning. Our plans for now are to go to the city, get a hotel room, and then meet up with some old friends that I worked with there. On Tuesday morning, we fly home. We will get a few days with Tim and Violet until they come home on Saturday."

James said, "I know we keep saying thank you for helping Kurt. I know it had cut into your time with the grandchildren. We will all plan to come visit you this year, a family at a time, to make up for those days you missed. The grandchildren love you and we need to get as much time together as a family as possible. Maybe you and Jean will consider coming back soon."

Back at the hotel, when Nick was in the shower, Jean returned Josephine's call. "Yes, Nick was trying to trick you into talking. I plan to tell him when it's all over but not now. It sounds like the end is tomorrow."

The two sisters discussed the plan, practiced the dialog and came up with alternative ideas. "Josephine, I really think you are right on with the plans for tomorrow. Make sure he doesn't see you get into a car. I know you have been taking all precautions with switching out license plates so the car and tags don't match up, and making sure he doesn't follow Deanie home. Also, remember to cancel the burner phone as soon as this is done. I don't believe there is a way to track it but I'm not a crook. I only see what is on TV, which isn't always true."

Josephine assured her, "We will be careful."

Outwood

Chapter 50 – Dealing with the DA (Monday)

The district attorney, Emily Anderson, came in with an attitude of a tough person. She opened to the defense attorney. "I plan to prosecute her as an adult. 17 is old enough to know better. I can't let someone off just because they are sorry now."

Amber entered with her parents. She was already a small person and very meek, but today she seemed every tinier. The DA was about to speak when Mr. Reddick burst through the door. "Before this get started, I'm the stepfather of the victim." The Prosecutor smiled thinking he would boost her belief in capital punishment but was surprised as he continued. "I really don't want charges brought against this young lady. She was friendly with my stepdaughter when we moved here. I know Amber and she is really a good person. I believe she was justified in her actions." By now, Emily's mouth was hanging open in shock. "Meredith did some nasty things to Amber's brother, Victor. She destroyed him to the point of him committing suicide. I didn't pay any attention to the girl back then. I had just married her mother and she was 16. I thought it was best to let her mother finish raising her. I was wrong, so very wrong. That girl destroyed many other people's lives, from spreading lies about them, setting them up to be embarrassed, or to take the fall from one of her deeds. Her malicious behavior caused me to lose a very high-paying, prestigious job and now they are causing her mother and I to divorce. When we moved into Outwood, we changed Meredith's name to hide from her past. We had no clue we were moving into the town Victor was from. I only knew him living in Boston. When Amber found out it was Meredith, now Julie, that did all those horrible things, who could blame her for her actions?"

Amber jumped up, "I didn't plan to kill her. I watched her do evil things to many people in town. If you went against her, she would spread lies about you. At first, I tried to be her friend and welcome her to our community, but then I found out she horrible she was. I was afraid of what she would do to me if I were to defy her. She cruelly embarrassed one of the boys at

SOCIAL DECEPTION MURDER

our school, tricking him into taking his clothes off and then shaming him for his build. She tried to get Kurt, a policeman in town, fired by telling lies that he made advances towards her. She wanted revenge for the speeding ticket. She offered sex to get let off, and when Kurt refused her, she went after him. Scott was her boyfriend, but he saw all the same things I did. He has a college scholarship and is good enough to have an NFL career. Julie saw herself being a part of that life but when he broke it off, he told everyone she ended it to help save face. It didn't stop her from attempting to destroy him. That night after hearing her plans for Scott and her past, I realized that she was really the Meredith Morrow that cause my brother to lose his law license, his career, and his life. Originally, I got the gun only to scare her, to make her see that she must stop. Instead, she talked about what losers my brother and I were and laughed at how she had hurt others. I'm sorry, I couldn't take it anymore. She already killed Victor and got away with it. I realized she could never be happy without hurting someone. If only you could have heard the words she shouted at me. I just couldn't take it. I might have destroyed my life, but at least I know how many other people I have saved. Whatever you do to me, I accept. I'm grateful I could save Kurt, Scott and the others." Amber sat down with her head in her arms and cried. Her parents wept quiet tears as well.

Amber's attorney gave a proposal of actions for mental help, confinement, and other steps in rehabilitation. Ms. Anderson looked over the proposal. "This is very expensive treatment at the places you proposed. Do you expect the state to pay for that?"

Mr. Reddick added, "The people Amber just listed is the tip of the iceberg of all the people Meredith had hurt. I'm paying for Amber's care if the court approves the plan and agrees to let me cover the cost. This family has suffered enough, first by losing their son, and now with what Amber is going through. It was my stepdaughter's fault. It's only right that I pay."

Ms. Anderson certainly changed her tune that she opened with. "I have never seen something like this where the victim's family is arguing for the accused. I'll agree with the plan. We will go to the judge together and get him to sign off on the decision."

Everyone left the room grateful. Amber ran into Nick and Jean's arms when she saw them in the hallway. Everyone else came over to join the hug, including Mr. Reddick.

Abletown

Chapter 51 – Confronting the Con Artist

Deanie sat at a table waiting for Wilson to come in. He smiled and rushed forward, "I'm so glad you are here. I was afraid you wouldn't come. Please tell me what's wrong. I care for you so much that I would do anything to make it right between us."

Josephine stepped out from behind a room divider, "I'm Della's daughter. I told her yesterday to cut it off with you. You came on a little too strong and I became suspicious. I checked you out and found out that you are a confidence man. You only wanted my mother for her money. She came today to hear the truth for herself."

MIA TENROC

Wilson jumped up. He had been sitting, holding Della's hand. "Who said those lies about me? I love your mother. I would never hurt her."

While they were talking, the families of the eight people that he had conned came quietly into the room. Josephine waved her hand to the back of the room. "Let's start with these good people."

Wilson turned and was shocked to see seven of his victims, with more people beside them. He dropped into his seat and took Della's hand. "I may have started calling on you in order to get money, but I really did fall in love with you. I never proposed marriage nor looked at rings with any of these ladies. I have changed."

Della stood and in an angry, shaky, tearful voice asked, "How can you live with yourself? All of this makes me feel cheap and sleazy." Della walked out of the room. Wilson looked crushed. Josephine walked out after her pretend mother.

A woman came forward. "I have your IOU for $12,500.00. If you have money in that briefcase, I suggest you repay me now."

Wilson retorted, "That's not my real name, so the IOU is no good." The woman reached for her cell phone and was dialing 911 when Wilson relented, "Ok, you are the only one with a valid claim. Here is your money." The suitcase was full. Each victim, surrounded by their family, came forward and he handed them the amount he had taken from them. Mr. Greenson was the last to approach. "I don't know who you are."

Mr. Greenson showed him the picture on his cell phone. Wilson instantly realized who this man was representing and handed him the money. Mr. Greenson coldly said, "While the money doesn't mean a thing to me, I will take it and use it to cover my expenses of tracking you. We have all agreed that you will never operate on the innocent again. We plan to work as a team to watch you 24/7. If you even talk to a woman, we will warn them of what you are. There are no words to express the contempt I feel for you. My mother died heartbroken. You killed her the same way as if you had used a knife on her."

Crushed and heartbroken, Wilson exited the restaurant and true to their word, he was followed by a chain of cars. He went into the boarding house to his room. Sick from grief, he went to bed. He got up and looked out the window many times throughout the day and night and found that there was always someone there; a different car many of the times, but always someone inside that he saw at the restaurant. He knew they would be tailing him for a few days but doubted it would last for long. He tried to call Della only to find her phone disconnected. He saw the irony of how his previous cons ended up preventing him from being with the one he actually loved. He had no other choice but to continue conning others to live, though his heart would never be in it the same way again. He returned to bed. All he wanted to do was sleep and forget.

Abletown

Chapter 52 – Returning to Abletown (Tuesday)

Jean was snuggled in Nick's arms. "I'm so glad this is all over. Definitely not the honeymoon I excepted, but at least we are together and alone at last."

Nick hated to destroy the mood but alas, they could no longer put off getting up if they wanted to catch the plane. "We better get up and head for the airport." In the car, Nick suggested, "We have a couple of hours driving ahead. This might be a good time to get that secret off your chest."

Jean teased, "It's not bothering me at all. I don't need to talk about it." After getting the reaction she expected, he knew there was no getting it out of her. "I will just touch the high points and then you can ask if you want to know more. This older woman died and at the funeral at Jake's place, her son showed a picture of a con man that pretended to be in love with her, milked as much money from her that he could get, then left her without even a goodbye. Mr. Greenson said his mother died of a broken heart. That night, Jake, Stacy, Alan and Naomi were out to dinner when they saw the crook with Priscilla."

Nick interjected, "It figures. Priscilla doesn't have good instincts about people. She would be an easy mark."

"She was handing the money over to the man, so Alan and Jake went up and prevented it. They told Priscilla about his usual deception. Instead of being grateful, she accused them of trying to ruin her happiness. Mr. Greenson had texted the picture of the con man, so Jake showed her. She grabbed her money back and left but still not believing in their good intentions. Fannie contacted her and got the information about the dating site and what had occurred in their relationship. Priscilla was asked not to post anything against the man they called Wilson Roberts until we gave her the word. We decided to do a reverse con on him." This earned Jean a dirty look. She ignored it and continued, "We tried to see who could play the victim. After some roleplaying with Deanie and Klaus, they felt that none of the other ladies could pull it off so Deanie decided it had to be her."

SOCIAL DECEPTION MURDER

"How could all of you do something so unsafe?" Nick was angry at this point. "That was a dangerous thing."

Jean assured him, "We covered all our bases. Deanie wore a mic and their conservations were recorded. There were always two people in the place with Deanie and there was a team in the van outside. We didn't let him figure out her address, and we drove different cars with the license plates switched so they would be difficult to trace. Meanwhile, Josephine and the others tracked down victims from his past. We found seven women that would admit to being conned and willing to come forth. They told us step-by-step the way the story would go. There was rehearsal for anything that might come up. As soon as he was hooked, Priscilla put out the warning and he took his profile off the dating sites. He claimed that he was a retired air force veteran who did charity flights now, and when it came time to asking for money, he would say that his daughter had to have surgery."

Nick nodded, "The bunco squad called him Slick Willie. There was always a "Wil" in either his first or last name. He's been around a long time, but he knows how to play things in a way that's not illegal."

Jean continued explaining the sting they pulled. "In the end, we were surprised because he actually fell in love with Deanie and wanted to marry her."

MIA TENROC

Nick laughed, "That was good acting."

Jean described the final day, "Many people got their money back. Deanie felt terrible for being so deceptive but understood how grateful the victims were. Wilson never knew that Deanie was playing him, so he won't be looking for her for revenge. The burner phone she used has now been disconnected, and her profile is gone. We think he will just leave town. He actually was very heartbroken, but I'm sure that didn't change him. I bet he'll go on suckering other innocent women to fall for him. At least some people got to tell him off and get their money back. We kept within the law. So, it's over now."

The flight home seemed to take forever. Tim and Violet picked them up at the airport with hugs and kisses. They went to Alan's game store and enjoyed the rest of the day.

At dinner that night at Nick's condo, Tim asked about the details of the case that Nick and Jean just solved. Jean allowed Nick to do all the talking and sat quietly. There was one thing that secretly bothered her: why did Amber take the boots? If Nick hadn't been so close to the situation, he would have questioned that detail. Jean thought there might have been more intent to pull the trigger than Amber had let on, but she was going to receive mental treatment and Julie got what she deserved. Jean decided that it was not up to her to

SOCIAL DECEPTION MURDER

ruin the happy ending that occurred. Some things are better left unsaid.

Tim appreciated all they did to clear Kurt. Nick said, "Your mother had quite the shock that someone would let her take a fall for murder. She thought everyone loved her and now realizes that she's the joke of the town. I don't know what their next step as husband and wife will be. Kurt is hurt and angry that his boss would arrest him. He is talking about looking for another job. Plus, they have to face the reality that they have no money. Not only that, but after hearing Amber's statement on her feelings toward them, particularly Sylvia, I doubt they can continue living across the street from the Johnson family."

Violet said, "I'm glad she now knows how disliked she is. I hope this will make her a nicer person. When we get home, I will call just to let her know how the honeymoon went. Maybe if I extend the olive branch, she will love us like a mother should."

Jean sat back looking at Violet proudly. She couldn't wait to get back to water aerobics to tell them what a wonderful daughter-in-law she was blessed with. They would discuss the two cases to make sure they handled everything the best way possible. Life would return to normal, quiet and boring but good. Nick asked that the team not do any more investigations again but they both knew more cases would come. Jean did promise to be more honest and tell Nick was going on. She hoped she could keep her word on that.

Turning in for the night, the family joined together for a family hug, each looking forward to another great day tomorrow.

Mia Tenroc

About the Author

Mia Tenroc started reading mysteries when she was 12 years old, Rex Stout and Agatha Christie being her favorites. She and her sister vowed to become mystery writers. Unable to work together, Mia designed the series with central characters that introduce each story in the first chapter but then each book is its own story. That way, she and her sister could write their own stories yet use these characters as the connection.

Mia's books are dedicated to demonstrating how what we say to one another really matters. She hopes to show that kind words build self-esteem and elevates people. A dedicated people watcher, Mia observes families interacting with each other which she uses as the basis for her books.

Mia tries to incorporate her small town into the books because there is a great joy in knowing your neighbors and being surrounded by family and friends. Mia loves to travel and experience the fun of seeing new place.

Made in the USA
Middletown, DE
01 December 2021